Every Wall a Ladder

John H. Johnson

Adapted by Quinn Currie

Storytellers Ink
Seattle, Washington

JB
Johnson
J
11/02
c/w

For my Mother

GERTRUDE JOHNSON WILLIAMS

without whom this story would not have been possible

FOREWORD

"Nobody succeeds alone or writes a book alone."

These are John Johnson's words written in 1989 in Chicago on the 50th Anniversary of the founding of Johnson Publishing Company, as he paid tribute to his family, his team of friends and employees, his subscribers, suppliers, and advertisers, all of whom played a part in his life, his work and his autobiography, *Succeeding Against the Odds*.

The founders of "Operation Outreach-USA" have selected John Johnson's life story as one of their "Light Up a Life" series books. It will be included in this nationally acclaimed program designed to develop literacy, character and compassion in students by providing training, instructions and free books to teachers and young adults.

John Johnson's inspirational life, with his dedication and courage as Johnny the boy grows into Johnson the man, will now be taught in schools across America using this adaptation of his autobiography.

Every Wall a Ladder, published on November 1, 1995, the fiftieth anniversary of his founding *Ebony* magazine, will be given free to teachers and students for years to come by sponsors, in hopes that it will positively affect the lives of all those who read and study it.

Contents

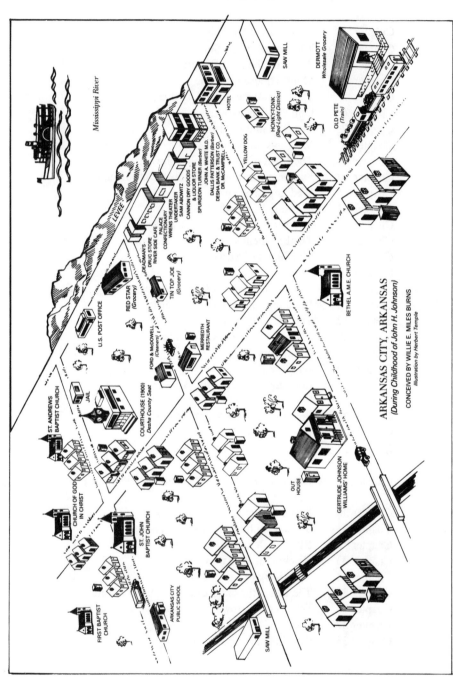

Map of my hometown, Arkansas City, Arkansas in the 1930s.

1
Two Against the Tide

We were running.

That's my first sharp memory.

We were running for our lives, and every living thing around us—man, woman, and child, dog, cat, and chicken, Black and White—was running, too.

The levee had broken, and the Mississippi River was on the rampage.

This was the message that greeted my mother and me as we emerged from St. John Baptist Church on Sunday, April 24, 1927.

We didn't know it then, but this was the beginning of the worst flood in American history; more than 800,000 Americans were running with us.

The first message said that the levee at Pendleton, twenty-five miles up the river from Arkansas City, had broken and that we should grab our valuables and run to the Arkansas City levee.

The second message, minutes later, said: Forget the valuables. Run for your lives!

And now we were running and the water was coming behind us and dogs were barking and people were screaming and my mother was gripping my hand so hard I thought it would come off.

Would we make it?

Or would the rampaging water roll over us, as it was rolling over the mules and chickens behind us?

For a terrifying moment, the issue was in doubt. Then my mother shifted into a higher gear, lifting me almost off the ground, and we scrambled up the slippery incline of the levee.

Hands. I remember the hands—black, white, brown, yellow hands—reaching out to us, pulling us to safety. And I remember, as if it were yesterday, the shock as I opened my eyes on a scene of pure bedlam.

By this time, six or seven hundred people and almost as many dogs were huddled together on the ridge, integrated in muddy misery. From time to time rabbits, quail, deer, and even foxes emerged from the water and scrambled over the man-made hills of furniture and clothes.

I stood for a moment, befuddled, shaking with excitement and fear.

I was nine years old, and I was standing in deep water that defined, annealed, baptized, and washed away.

But none of that was clear to me, as I lifted my face to the rain.

Above everything else, above dignity and happiness and all hopes for the future, was the question of survival.

We were two—a Black boy and a Black woman—against the tide. Would we—could we—survive against such odds? And what would happen to me if my mother and I were separated or—God forbid—if she suffered some mishap?

The question was a nightmare that pressed in on me, like a load of sandbags, and interfered with my breathing and made the ground shake beneath my feet. There were other fears, more immediate, more pressing. The fear I shared with almost everybody, the fear of the big nasty slithering snakes—moccasins and blue runners—that oozed out of the water and hid in the bundles and tents.

This was one side of the coin. The other side, the lure of excitement and adventure, also pressed in on me. I soon perceived that there were things to be seen on this levee that a nine-year-old boy had never seen.

With the help of Blacks and Whites, who paid no attention to our color, we settled on the island of the levee, where we lived for six weeks. On one side was "Ol' Man River," not the romantic river of the song but an arrogant monster, constantly probing and looking for a weak spot in the circle of sandbags. On the other side was a new body of water where Arkansas City used to be.

From the vantage point of the levee, I watched the water cover the tin roof of our home.

It is one of the peculiarities of the mind that it magnifies trivialities in moments of tragedy. I was overwhelmed at that moment by the thought that my favorite toy was gone and that I would never see it again. It didn't occur to me until later that we were naked in the world and that everything we owned— our clothes, our furniture, and the few dollars we'd saved—was gone.

This, then, was the beginning of a new beginning. We were new people in a new world, Noahs without arks.

Frederick Simpich, a writer for the *National Geographic* magazine, wrote, "At noon the streets of Arkansas City were dry and dusty. By two o'clock, mules were drowning in the main streets of that town faster than they could be unhitched from wagons. Before dark the homes and stores stood six feet deep in water."

Before it was over, twenty feet of water covered Arkansas City, and parts of seven southern states were inundated in what President Herbert Hoover called "the greatest peace-time disaster in our history."

I was too young to understand all of the implications of what I saw. But it was a revelation to me that the Mississippi River had washed away the sin of division, and that Blacks and Whites were working together fighting the Mississippi together, shoulder-to-shoulder.

The Negroes of Arkansas City, my family among them, were outstanding workers, manning the shovels, throwing the sandbags, patching the cuts, pacing themselves, measuring themselves, pleasuring themselves by the steady, rhythmic beat of their songs.

I'm so glad—hunh!
That trouble don't last always.
It lasted long enough.

And when we picked our way through the mud, keeping a sharp eye out for snakes, to the site of our house, we found another trouble. The house was gone, and that pleased us. The authorities had promised to build new homes for families who couldn't find their old houses. But we were unlucky. We found

3

our old house three blocks away, battered and full of dirt and nameless things that crawled and slithered.

And so it started again, the rhythm of our lives.

My parents and my parents' parents had lived in this valley for generations, building the levees to contain the River, fleeing in panic after the inevitable flood overturned years of hard work, cleaning up and starting over after the flood, building new homes, new lives, new dreams, and waiting, waiting, waiting, always waiting and living on the edge for the next warning, the next flood, and the next rush to high ground.

This was the rhythm of my people, of the Johnsons and the Jenkinses, who'd lived on the banks of the Mississippi for generations.

They knew the River, the Johnsons and Jenkinses.

They loved it, hated it, feared it.

The River was in their souls.

It was their destiny, their fate, their curse.

I never hear Langston Hughes's poem without wondering about that long line of Johnsons and Jenkinses and the inner resources that made it possible for them to survive their struggle with the River that dominated and controlled their lives.

I've known rivers:
I've known rivers ancient as the world and older than the
flow of human blood in human veins.
My soul has grown deep like the rivers.
I bathed in the Euphrates when dawns were young.
I built my hut near the Congo and it lulled me to sleep.
I looked upon the Nile and raised the pyramids above it.
I heard the singing of the Mississippi when Abe Lincoln
went down to New Orleans, and I've seen its muddy
bosom turn all golden in the sunset.
I've known rivers:
Ancient, dusky rivers.
My soul has grown deep like the rivers.

2
The Heritage of a Survivor

The Johnsons and Jenkinses were old southern families who came to America from Africa. By the time of the Great Flood of 1927, they had known rivers, blood, sweat, tears, joy, slavery, and emancipation.

This saga of survival was too personal, too *real* to my mother, who never talked about it. But to the children and grandchildren of slavery, slavery was pain in the flesh, horror in the mind, nightmares in the night.

They were still living it. They were bound hand and foot by the infamous sharecropping system. And survivors of slavery, like King Banks, my mother's stepfather, were living reminders. It is no wonder that they didn't talk about it and that the children of the third generation of freedom had to find their own road to the past and to the future.

I found my own way and distilled a vague and yet painfully sharp image of the Johnson-Jenkins past. Somewhere in a vague place called Africa—I had no idea, in my youth, where it was or how to get there—the first Johnson and Jenkins were captured, chained, branded, and put into the hold of a slave ship for the trip to America.

Millions of fellow citizens—they were Africans, sons and daughters of the builders of the Pyramids and great empires—died on the slave ships, where they were packed so close together that they couldn't move, and on the plantations, where they worked from sunup to sundown for two hundred years. But millions more, the Jenkinses and Johnsons among them, survived.

I am their son and descendant.

And I am a survivor, too.

Survival is in my blood. It's in my nerves and muscles. For I am a descendant of people who were so tough that nothing—neither slavery, nor segregation, nor the River—could destroy them.

In the end, by some mystery no historian can truly explain, the first Johnson-Jenkins not only survived but prevailed and was reborn on the banks of the Mississippi River in the person of Gertrude Jenkins, who came into this world on Tuesday, August 4, 1891, in Lake Village, Arkansas. Her parents were two young Arkansans, Will and Malinda Jenkins. They were born after slavery. My mother, therefore, was of the second generation of freedom.

This was not a good time for a Black girl to be born. The 1890s were, by all accounts, the low point on the graph of Black life in America. This was the decade of Jim Crow laws and almost daily lynchings.

During this decade and the first decades of the twentieth century, the Ku Klux Klan and other violent organizations reversed the Fourteenth and Fifteenth amendments and drove Black businessmen from downtown sections in Little Rock. At the same time, violent men destroyed the electoral foundation of politicians like R. C. Weddington, who represented Desha County and Arkansas City in the Arkansas legislature in 1891.

They would write books about this in the twentieth century, but it was no theory to young Gertrude Jenkins, who lived the death of Black hope. By means we can only imagine, she completed the third grade. She was then driven—by poverty, by need, by want—into the fields and kitchens of the Mississippi Valley. But she always lived in a valley on the other side of oppression. Her body was in the fields and kitchens but her mind was never captive and never lingered there. She knew exactly what she wanted out of life and passed it on to her son.

Always hopeful, always cheerful, she settled in Arkansas City, where she worked as a domestic and became active in the church and service organizations.

In the first decades of the century, Arkansas City was a growing, rip-roaring Mississippi River town built around a thriving sawmill. In those days, the city was a transportation terminal, and people came from Little Rock, from Pine Bluff, from all over, to catch the ferry to Mississippi.

Overshadowing Front Street, a single row of business houses, and two major buildings, the Desha County Courthouse and the three-story Desha Bank, was the towering Mississippi River levee. There were separate-but-equal honky-tonks on the riverfront in the Yellow Dog section.

For churchgoing people and culture lovers, there were excursions on the Mississippi and a theater on Front Street. Out on Highway 4 there was an arena which seated some 2,500 people. In 1924, Jack Dempsey, the heavy-weight champion of the world, fought here in an exhibition.

The major town landmark was the big clock on the tower of the Desha County Courthouse. The courthouse and the clock have a tragic and ghostly history. According to stories that were told over and over in Black households, a Black was lynched on the courthouse grounds in the first decade of the century.

The victim maintained his innocence to the end. Before he died, he put a curse on the courthouse, saying the clock would never tell the correct time again. To the dismay of Whites, the clock had erratic tendencies, and the hands finally stuck at five o'clock, where they remain to this day.

In this setting, in the shadow of the clock, Gertrude Jenkins met and married Richard Lewis and gave birth to her first child, a daughter named Beulah. The marriage didn't work, and "Miss Gert," as almost everybody called my mother, later married Leroy Johnson, a handsome laborer who worked in the sawmill and helped out on the levee.

I was born to this couple on Saturday, January 19, 1918, shortly after midnight, in a shotgun, tin-roofed house about three blocks from the river. My mother didn't name me John, as is commonly believed. I was christened "Johnny" Johnson because my mother had promised a close friend, Johnnie Ford, that she would name her next child Johnny (or Johnnie), whether she had a boy or a girl.

I was born in the last year of World War I, the war that made the world safe for democracy, triggered the Great (Black) Migration to the North and changed Black and White America forever.

In the first years of my life, an armistice ended World War I, the first Pan-African Congress met, Madame C. J. Walker died, Liberty Life Insurance Company was incorporated, and troops put down the Chicago riot. These were also the launching years of Model T and Model A Fords, the Charleston, the Black Bottom, flappers, jazz, movies, and the radio.

It was in this America, in a segregated and restricted environment bounded by the Mississippi River and the St. John Baptist Church on the east and the Arkansas City Colored School on the west, that I spent the first fifteen years of life.

They were years of struggle, wonder, and growth, cushioned by a close-knit family and a close-knit community. One of the ironies of our situation is that progress, urbanization, and decades of unemployment destroyed the foundations of the strong Black community that enabled Blacks to survive slavery and segregation.

I was lucky.

I was born into a strong family and reared in a strong community where every Black adult was charged with the responsibility of monitoring and supervising every Black child. I was reared in a community where every Black adult was authorized to whip me, if I needed whipping, and to send me home for a second whipping from my mother.

I was a nonsmoker and nondrinker who was born into poverty. I grew up in a small southern town and was reared by strong and loving parents who spared neither hugs nor rods.

Is there a message in this?

Yes. The message is that we've strayed in Black America—and in White America—from the values of family, community, and hard work. And we've got to go back to that culture. We've got to go back to the time when being an adult was a demanding vocation that required a total commitment to the community and every child in it.

My mother was a disciplinarian who used a "switch," as she called it, to emphasize her teaching. At bottom-line time, she'd make me go into the backyard and cut a switch or branch from a tree. I always cut a small one, and she always sent me back to get a bigger and stronger branch. In later years people asked me why I never smoked cigarettes or drank whiskey. I never smoked or drank because my mother caught me smoking behind the house when I was ten and gave me a beating that I remember to this day.

But we must be careful here. For beating alone will not improve the manners of mules or men. The solution here and elsewhere is toughness leavened by the dough of love.

I didn't have a lot of toys. I didn't have a lot of clothes. But I had a lot of love.

I spent most of my formative years as the only child in a two-parent household. My half sister, Beulah, who was fourteen years older, left home to teach school in a neighboring town when I was small. My mother's cousin, Willie Miles, stayed with us a year or two, but she, too, moved on to Little Rock and institutions of higher learning.

I was reared in two-parent households, but there was never any doubt: my mother was the dominant force in the household and in my life. She was a short, forceful woman then, not quite five feet, with the family bowlegs and a big smile and a will of steel. She walked straight up, her head held high, a woman of stature and quality. She had known pain and discouragement and fear. Out of all this came a special kind of dignity. The dignity of a person who'd seen a lot and survived and wasn't afraid of the future.

In another day, my mother would have been a politician or a leader. She was always organizing clubs and service organizations. And she excelled in the most difficult of all American politics, the politics of the Black church. The churches she belonged to were always fussing and fighting about the election of pastors and the distribution of church property, and she almost always ended up on the winning side.

My father, on the other hand, was an outgoing man who didn't, according to my mother, take family responsibilities seriously. He was about five feet eleven with dark brown skin. He had a beautifully groomed mustache which I admired and which I emulate to this day.

I never really knew him. He traveled a lot, following the levee camps up and down the Mississippi. He was killed in a sawmill accident when I was eight. The next year, the year of the flood, my mother married James Williams, who delivered groceries for a bakery shop. He was a good stepfather, and we never had a cross word.

This was, in part, the doing of my mother. She told us if we had anything pleasant to say to each other we should communicate directly. But if we had anything unpleasant to say, we should tell her and she, in turn, would tell the offending party.

Even if we were in the same room, I would say, "Mother, tell Mr. Williams to stop doing that." And he would say, "Gertrude, tell Johnny I don't like that." Some people thought this routine was funny. The only thing I can say is that it worked—for thirty-four years.

3
Race and the
First Picture Show

I was a working child.

I learned how to work before I learned how to play. When most children were experimenting with their first toys, I was hard at work in the real world, helping my mother and stepfather.

My stepfather, like my real father, moonlighted on the Mississippi, following the levee camps and pitching in during floods. My mother oftentimes accompanied him, washing and ironing clothes for the laborers and cooking in the levee kitchens. I tagged along and learned at an early age how to cook and how to wash and iron clothes. Even when my mother did day work, I went along and ran errands.

Despite, or perhaps because of this early labor, I was, in the words of my mother, "a hell-raiser." I loved a prank, a good joke, and a fish fry. I also had an eye for girls. But Arkansas City, unfortunately, was not fertile ground for fantasy or, given the close watch of my mother and other adults, experimentation. Most of the boys had a secret crush on Willie B. Frazier, the daughter of the town's richest Black, but she paid little or no attention to us.

Was I happy?

The question has no meaning. Happiness is a concept based on a comparison. And we had no basis for comparison. Arkansas City was our whole world. There was the sawmill factory and the levee and the River, and beyond that—nothing. There were no newspapers or radios. We thought the way we lived was the way people were supposed to live.

We didn't have money, but we weren't—crucial distinction—poor. Our poverty, in other words, couldn't be compared with the soul-crushing poverty in the slums of modern America.

I was never hungry. When my mother worked as a domestic, she cooked more than she served, and White families let her bring food home. She usually worked for families with children, and I got their old clothes.

Did this bother me? Not at first. I had been conditioned to believe that this was the way things were supposed to be. I had shoes and pants. In the winter we had heat. In the summer the iceman brought ice. On hot Sundays, we cranked the old freezer and made ice cream and sat on the front porch and fanned ourselves.

It was not a *completely* bad life. The only problem, dim at first but constantly growing clearer, was a feeling that we were not in control of our destiny, that a word or a frown from a White person could change our plans and our lives.

What we now call race relations were generally peaceful. Blacks and Whites lived next door to each other, and there were few instances of outright brutality in my youth. We were right across the river from Mississippi, and we heard horror stories about lynchings. There was one story in particular about a Black man who was lynched for winking at a White woman. We didn't believe that sort of thing could happen in Arkansas City. But to prevent any misunderstanding we made a conscious effort not to blink our eyes in the presence of a White woman.

My mother, like the mothers of other southern Black sons, shielded me from segregation and discrimination. She was always saying, "Don't do that!" "Don't say that!" As a result, I never really confronted the system. Yet I always knew that I was different, and that I was in danger.

I was ten or eleven when I came face to face with the bared fangs of the system. My mother was working for a wealthy doctor, who sent me to the drugstore to pick up a prescription. When I got to the store on a hot Saturday afternoon, one of the clerks asked, "What do you want, nigger?"

He put so much venom into the word that I ran, crying, to my mother. She told the doctor, who went downtown and shook the clerk until his teeth rattled and said, in effect: "Don't you call *my* nigger a nigger."

It was important in that era for a Black family to have a

kind of "protective custody" relationship with a strong and important White family. If you worked for such a family, the head of the family would protect you from other Whites. He didn't always protect you from himself or members of his family, but he protected you from others.

The funniest—and saddest—incidents of this period grew out of attempts to control the laughing of Black people. When the first picture show came to town, the first floor was reserved for Whites, and Blacks were assigned to the balcony. Blacks were also told, in so many words, that we could only laugh when White people laughed.

If, as often happened, a scene set off an uproar in the Black section, someone would say, "You niggers, cut out that laughing." The laughing would die down, with a few impudent snickers, until a scene struck the fancy of the White audience and there was a general license for Blacks to laugh along with the Whites.

But it never really worked. For Blacks, as a form of defiance or film criticism, always laughed too long and too loud, bringing forth the command, "You niggers, cut out that laughing!" I'm glad there were no Richard Pryor movies in that era, for some Blacks would have literally laughed themselves to death.

4
Many Thousands Gone

Despite the usual racial problems, Arkansas City was a cut above the typical southern town. A Black doctor, John A. White, was in the main office building. Another Black, Dallas Patterson, operated a barbershop in the same building.

One of my early heroes was Paris Frazier, a levee contractor and carpenter who dominated the building trade and constructed houses for Blacks and Whites. Frazier, the first Black in town to own a car, lived in a palatial house by Arkansas City standards. It had an indoor toilet, an unheard-of luxury in that day. When we played with his daughter, Willie, we used to flush the toilet and wonder where the waste went.

I decided that I wanted a house like that and a shiny car that kicked up dust in the road and an indoor toilet that flushed.

We arrive, by means of an indoor toilet, at a crucial educational principle. People are pretty much the same everywhere. Black, white, brown, yellow, magenta, they only see what they see. They only reach for what they can reach. They only struggle, to paraphrase Frederick Douglass, when there is a reasonable chance of whipping somebody or some thing. It takes an unusual person like my mother to believe what can't be seen and to stake everything on a card that has never fallen.

I shared my mother's faith. I believed in the plastic power of the possible. I believed with her that the possible, the thing that can be, is greater than the actual.

But a little hard evidence never hurt any true believer. And Paris Frazier's car and indoor toilet were concrete motivations that were more persuasive than a thousand lectures and sermons. The only thing I knew was that I wanted something different from the dirt, sweat, and pain around me.

For two or three years, I played a private game, putting on different robes and roles. I abandoned the Paris Frazier model, not because of the overalls, but because I knew nothing about carpentry and saw no immediate chance to learn. I was attracted, however, to the ministry for a lot of reasons.

The minister was one of the few Blacks in our community who wore a suit and had the respect of Blacks and Whites. He also had the pick of the chicken pieces at Sunday dinners.

I studied the preacher, imitated his movements, and listened carefully to the sermons, hoping one day to duplicate what he was doing. Since I spent all day Sunday in church, it was easy to pursue my studies. My mother took me to Sunday School on Sunday morning and we stayed for church. After dinner, we returned for BYPU, Baptist Young People's Union, and the night services.

There was a strict line of division in Arkansas City between "good" people who attended church and frowned on drinking and honky-tonking, and the "bad" people who gambled and visited the hot spots.

My mother was on the good side. My father and stepfather were ecumenical. My vote was cast by proxy by my mother and her switch.

I decided finally that my long range hope was in the Arkansas City Colored School. The school was run by a legendary principal, C. S. Johnson, a graduate of Atlanta Baptist College (now Morehouse), and his wife, M. J. Johnson, a graduate of Spelman.

Professor Johnson, like most pioneer Black teachers, taught everything: reading, writing, arithmetic, manners. He inspected our clothes to make sure we were neat and clean, and insisted on polished shoes and correct behavior. He was, in fact, an extension of the home. Like my mother, like most Arkansas City parents, he carried a big stick and used it.

Although the four-room school was somewhat primitive by modern standards, it stressed excellence and brought better results than most contemporary schools. There was no nonsense in this building. We knew that education for us was a matter of life and death, and that certain graduates of this school, including my half sister, Beulah, and my cousin, Willie, had climbed out of their dungeons on a ladder of words.

Always, everywhere, by work, by example, by the carrot and stick, Professor Johnson pressed this message: What they did, you can and *must* do, too.

The only problem was that the Arkansas City Colored School System stopped at the eighth grade. If I intended to get out of my dungeon, I had to find a new or a longer ladder.

This was the consuming passion of my life in the late twenties and thirties. In 1930, when work ran out in Arkansas City, my stepfather joined a levee camp upriver, and my mother took me to Vicksburg, Mississippi, to live with a family she knew. I went to St. Mary's Catholic School for a year and then returned to Arkansas City for the eighth and final grade.

By this time, cracks were developing in the towering levee of race. You could see this clearly in the militant *Chicago Defender* newspapers that Black Pullman porters smuggled into nearby McGehee. These newspapers, which reported the opportunities developing in Chicago and other northern cities, gave me an intellectual and physical thrill. I loved to touch the newsprint and trace the contours of the screaming red headlines. I didn't know it until later, but I had been called—and found.

There were other cracks in the dam. One of my mother's childhood friends, Mamie Johnson, migrated to the big city of Chicago like millions of other Blacks. She sent letters to friends and relatives, and in one to my mother said armies of Blacks were flocking to Chicago. There, education, good jobs, and freedom were ours for the asking.

This was a historic movement similar in tone and texture to the nineteenth-century flight of the slaves, who sang a famous song:

No more peck of corn for me.
No more, no more.
No more peck of corn for me.
Many thousands gone.

Many thousands were gone and going. This was a new and interesting fact, and I looked at myself and my world with different eyes. I took this new thing that was stirring in me up to the levee and looked out over the Mississippi River and wondered what was happening in the great world beyond and whether God had a place in it for me.

5
The Advantage
of the Disadvantage

There is an advantage in every disadvantage, and a gift in every problem.

My disadvantage—one that carried me to unprecedented heights—was that Arkansas City didn't provide a high school education for Blacks. I've thanked fate for that gift many times. For if there had been a high school for Blacks in Arkansas City, I would have attended it, and I would not have left for Chicago and the wonders that lay in my future.

My second disadvantage was an economic crunch, stemming from the Great Depression. This crunch eliminated the traditional Black option of sending a boy or girl to boarding school in Pine Bluff or Little Rock.

These two disadvantages were simple facts which couldn't by themselves motivate anybody. They became a problem when they were integrated into the lives of a boy and his mother, who decided that they were challenges to be overcome and not facts to be passively accepted.

It was this problem that transformed my life. For, from my perspective, God, history, fate, life—choose a word—was challenging me, *testing* me, offering me prizes beyond my wildest imagination when I was faced with what looked like an impassable wall.

There was nothing magical or unique about this situation. There comes a moment in every person's life when he or she stands faced with a choice, one of which leads up and over and the other down and out. And the choice they make at that moment defines them forever.

There were two choices, and two choices only, before me, and I had to choose. The choice, as usual, was between security and insecurity, between the known and the unknown. I had to decide whether I was going to hang on to the devil I knew or whether I was going to turn loose, without a safety net, and free-fall to danger, destiny, wealth, or death.

I've believed ever since that living on the edge, living in and through your fear, is the summit of life, and that people who refuse to take that dare condemn themselves to a life of living death.

With the help of my mother, who instinctively understood all this, I chose danger, destiny, and wealth. The choice was not easy. For when I entered the last grade of the Arkansas City Colored School in the fall of 1931, it seemed that I had exhausted all my options and that I was condemned to live a life of drudgery on the banks of this river in the shadow of a clock that had stopped running.

But this appraisal didn't take into consideration the fierce Dream of a mother, who had another and better idea. This is how we changed our fate and made a ladder out of a wall.

The first step, as always, was to redefine the situation so we would have the initiative and would understand clearly what we had to do. This meant that we had to study the battleground and understand the strength and weaknesses of the opposing forces. We knew—how could we help knowing?—that all the high ground and money and weapons were in the hands of our adversaries. But it was worse than useless in that day to grind our teeth and curse racism. The question, the only question, was what were we going to do with what we had to make things better for ourselves.

If I had to identify the most important step in a strategy of success, I would pick that question. The basic problem for a young man or woman is not what other people are going to do, but what *you* are going to do.

Seen from this perspective, the situation presented new and even exciting possibilities. There was no Black public high school in Arkansas City. But Arkansas City, according to the *Chicago Defender* and letters we received from the North, was not the whole world. There were Black public high schools in Chicago and other northern cities. Millions of Blacks had migrated to the North to take advantage of this. And we were "free" to join them if we could save the money to pay for the train tickets.

There were other weapons in our small arsenal. My mother's childhood friend Mamie Johnson had married "a railroad man"—Blacks who worked on the railroad were among the elite in old Black communities. The Johnsons had bought a three-flat building on Chicago's South Side. Mrs. Johnson had written several letters to my mother, suggesting that we move to Chicago and stay with her until we could get our feet on the ground. To make things even more interesting and inviting, my half sister, Beulah, was planning to move to Chicago, too.

So there it was. Forget, for a moment, the NAACP and the Great Depression. Forget the state of Arkansas and segregated schools. Forget Franklin Delano Roosevelt and the New Deal. The only relevant question here was what were Gertrude Johnson Williams and her son, Johnny, going to do about this situation.

When we posed that question and broke it down into steps based on the direct alternatives open to us, we changed and the problem changed.

But it looks simpler now than it did then. For as I made my way through the eighth and final grade of the Arkansas City Colored School, the economic situation deteriorated, making the Dream of hundreds of thousands of Black men and women, including my stepfather, migrant workers, the Dream of Gertrude Johnson Williams, of taking her boy to the city where he could get a decent education and become somebody, recede, like the fickle water of the Mississippi.

We intended to leave for Chicago in 1932, immediately after my graduation from grade school. But when I graduated in June 1932, there wasn't enough money in the secret bank under the mattress to go to Little Rock, much less to Chicago.

This didn't faze my mother, who redoubled her efforts, cooking, washing, and ironing for whole camps of levee workers, and volunteering for every extra job that came up. During the whole of this summer, she was like a woman possessed. So was I. I shared the feverish hours, washing and ironing clothes

19

and cooking meals for as many as fifty men. I became, in fact, a master cook and developed a fondness for certain dishes that I prepare even today. French-fried sweet potatoes, for example, and a Johnson specialty, steak and pork chops cut into small pieces, seasoned and simmered in a gravy, and served over rice.

It quickly became apparent we weren't going to have enough money to travel to Chicago before the beginning of the school season. It was at this moment that my mother gave me some astonishing news: I was going to return to Arkansas City School and repeat the eighth grade. She didn't want me running wild on the streets, she said. And she didn't want me to get used to a life of menial work. To prevent that, I was going to repeat the eighth grade two, three, four times—as many times as necessary.

"You're going to stay in the eighth grade," she said, "until we've got enough money to go to Chicago." This was not at all palatable to a sensitive young boy who had to go back to his old school and sit in the same room with younger boys and girls.

People laughed at us, not for the first or the last time. Neighbors told my mother that she was crazy to make sacrifices for a boy who would never amount to anything anyway. My mother said nothing. She kept on working and dreaming and saving.

She'd always believed that there was a solution to every problem, and that the solution was in God's hands, not human hands. But she believed also, and with equal fervor, that God helped those who helped themselves. As the catcalls and criticisms mounted, she told me to pay no attention to the doubters. "Victory," she said, "is certain if we have the courage to believe and the strength to run our own race."

The taunts came from the outside and were painful but bearable. But my mother had a different and heavier cross to bear. For my stepfather also doubted the wisdom of the planned move. There was no hostility in his opposition. He simply lacked the breadth of imagination to conceive the merits of the plan.

This argument poisoned life in the little house near the

levee. It was there in the grits of breakfast. It seasoned the pork chops at dinner and the long stretches of silence in between. All that time—for more than a year—my mother never wavered, never looked back.

When, in July of 1933, the last sweat-soaked dollar was added to the pile, she turned her face to the North and freedom.

In a last desperate effort to keep us in Arkansas City, my stepfather played his trump card, saying we were traveling to disaster, we were going to stand in unemployment lines in the cold Chicago wind and freeze to death in the winter.

Looking back now and knowing how deeply my mother cared for my stepfather, I think this was one of the most courageous acts of her life: leaving her husband, the man she dearly loved, in Arkansas City, and embarking with me on this journey, not knowing how long we would survive in a strange city.

Her heart may have been broken, but she never wavered as we climbed into the makeshift bus—a private car operated by enterprising neighbors—for the trip to the train station in McGehee, twelve miles away. She loved my stepfather, but loved freedom and education more.

This was one of the biggest moments of my life, and I'm ashamed to admit that I remember neither the hour nor the day. But there is a wisdom in the body that is older and more reliable than clocks and calendars.

And that July day is engraved in the calendar of my nerves. I can see it now, and taste it: the fierce Arkansas sun, the rivers of sweat running down my back, the smell of fried chicken and potato salad and marble cake in the brown paper bags. And the steam and the roar of the monster train—was there ever a sweeter and more terrifying sound to a boy?—and the stirring words "All aboard!" and all the way to Little Rock, all the way to Memphis, all the way up the River to St. Louis, the beating of my heart, and the hot, cinder-filled ambiance of the Jim Crow railroad car.

I was feverish with excitement, with fear, with hope.

It was July 1933.

I was fifteen years old.

Nothing would ever be the same again.

6
Goin' to Chicago

Chicago was to the southern Blacks of my generation a Mecca, a Jerusalem, a city of magic on which we focused all of our dreams.

Millions of Black southerners migrated to Harlem, Detroit, Pittsburgh, Gary, and Philadelphia, but Chicago was a special place of special and sassy Blacks who were making legends and doing things they didn't do on Broadway or anywhere else.

Between 1900 and 1930 the Chicago Black population increased five times to 234,000. In this period, millions of Blacks migrated to northern cities in a movement that was as significant in its implications as the international movement that brought millions to Ellis Island.

The Ellis Island story has been endlessly related and immortalized. Not enough attention has been given to the saga of the Blacks who came up from the South with all their hopes, fears, and flimsy cardboard suitcases.

These internal immigrants changed the beat of America. They brought the blues with them and jazz and gospel music. They brought the rhythms and styles that changed Broadway and American music and culture.

Day after day, week after week, and then month after month, all through the twenties, thirties, and forties, the Black migrants came in the biggest migration in American history. The first big wave (300,000) came between 1910 and 1920, followed by a second wave (1.3 million) between 1920 and 1930. The third and fourth waves, even larger, came in the thirties (1.5 million) and the forties (2.5 million). 40,000 southern Blacks came to Chicago in the thirties.

Gertrude Johnson Williams and her son were of the class of 1933.

Like millions of other migrants, we followed the curve of the River, going from Little Rock to Memphis to St. Louis to Chicago. For most of the journey, my face was pressed so tight against the window that I could hardly breathe. I was captivated by the tall buildings, motorcars, and bright lights. I wanted to get off in Little Rock. I wanted to get off in Memphis. I had to be physically restrained in St. Louis.

When, late at night, we finally arrived at the Illinois Central Station at Twelfth Street and Michigan Avenue, I stood transfixed on the street. I had never seen so many Black people before. I had never seen so many tall buildings and so much traffic.

The Illinois Central Station no longer stands, which is a historical calamity. The building should have been preserved to commemorate the millions who poured through its portals in search of the same dream as the Ellis Island immigrants. Although they were native to the land and spoke the same language, the barriers the Black migrants faced were at least as difficult. And their struggle, which continues even today, was and is equally courageous.

A taxi took us to a narrow, three-story building where mother's friend Mamie Johnson warmly greeted us. She'd made a bedroom for us out of the third-floor attic. Mother slept in the bed and I slept on a rollaway bed.

Before closing my eyes on that first night I inspected the steam heat and the inside toilet. I was greatly impressed with Chicago. I knew it was going to be my kind of town.

My mother quickly found a job as a domestic, making three or four dollars a day and carfare. And as soon as we could, we rented a room in the same apartment building as my half sister, Beulah, who'd moved to Chicago shortly before our arrival and helped us make the transition to big-city life.

Beulah was a brilliant and complex woman, a former teacher who'd mastered the dressmaking trade and was employed in the garment district.

Black Chicago, then and now, was a city within a city and in many ways the best school available for a Black boy of my age and situation. Tough, brutal, unforgiving, it lived on the edge. It challenged you, provoked you, and dared you.

Fate did me a favor by sending me to the city with the best

Black politicians and businessmen. Black Chicagoans had a history of political and economic independence going back to Jean Baptiste Pointe du Sable, the Black man who founded the city. I learned later at DuSable High School that the Potawatomi Indians used to smile and say, "The first white man to settle in 'Checagou' was a black man."

Building on that history, Black men and women made Chicago a political and economic beacon.

There was a fundamental difference between White Chicago and Black Chicago. For the Black world was organized around rituals and institutions that were virtually unknown on Lake Shore Drive.

Not State Street but the great street of South Parkway (now Dr. Martin Luther King Jr. Drive) dominated Black Chicago. The street ran like a concrete river through the heart of the South Side. It linked my home with Wendell Phillips High School, the South Parkway and the Thirty-fifth Street business district, where all of the major Black companies had their headquarters. Nearby at Thirty-fifth and Indiana, was the *Chicago Defender* office.

All roads of Black Chicago ran into South Parkway, a great big picture-book street with at one point five lanes of traffic in each direction. There was a tree-lined oasis in the middle of the street and two-and three-story houses and apartment buildings of every imaginable color and texture on both sides.

I would walk in later years down the Champs-Elysées and I would ride in a chauffeur-driven limousine down Fifth Avenue. But there was never another street, in fact or in fiction, to compare with the grand boulevard that dazzled the eyes of a fifteen-year-old boy in 1933.

From my arrival until the establishment of my first business, South Parkway was my home base and the center of my world. A few blocks to the east was the shimmering sea of Lake Michigan, which contrasted so strongly with the muddy Mississippi of my youth.

In addition to "Policy" millionaires, wealthy and militant publishers, jazz players, blues singers, ball players, hustlers,

24

businessmen, surgeons, and lawyers, Chicago had political leaders who could hold their own in what was even then the most exciting political theater in America.

Of all the people I met in this early period, Oscar DePriest was easily the most outstanding. He was the first Black Congressman from the North and the first Black in Congress since the Reconstruction period. Not only did he talk like a congressman but he looked and acted like one.

In September 1933, I was scrubbed to within an inch of my life and sent to Wendell Phillips, a virtually all-Black high school named for the White abolitionist hero.

Because of a cultural misunderstanding, I immediately gained an advantage. When I entered the school on my first day, I found students milling around the registration desks, yelling "1A!" "2A!" and "2B!" Not wanted to appear stupid, I picked a number out of the air and said "2." Nobody challenged me, and I skipped the ninth grade and started in the second year of high school. This was poetic justice since I was probably the only person in the world with two eighth-grade diplomas.

I enrolled in a general language course with a heavy emphasis in civics. Since I wanted to be a journalist, I also enrolled in a journalism course and signed up for work on the school newspaper, the *Phillipsite*. I later became editor-in-chief of the paper and sales manager of the school yearbook, the *Red and Black*.

This was the fulfillment of a childhood dream. I'd been in love with newspapers and newspaper people since my first encounter with the *Chicago Defender* in Arkansas City.

To this day, I'm a compulsive magazine and newspaper buyer who can't pass a newsstand without stopping. That's the first stop I make in every city I visit. I want to see what's available. I want to touch the newsprint and glossy paper and feel through them the pulse and the heartbeat of the community.

It's not surprising, therefore, that I majored in journalism with a related interest in civics. Many of my classmates believed that I would follow my second love, law. The class prophecy said "Attorney General John H. Johnson" would successfully represent the government.

Nothing in my experience had prepared me for Wendell Phillips, which had a student population larger than the total population of Arkansas City. So many students were enrolled— more than 3,000 in 1933—that there were double and triple shifts, and portable classrooms.

Chicago was up North, but it was rigidly segregated. The student body was almost totally Black, but the principal and most of the teachers were White. The assistant principal was a Black woman, Mrs. Annabel Carey Prescott.

The physical presence of Mrs. Prescott and other Black teachers and administrators was more important than the lessons they taught. I'd never seen so many well-dressed and well-educated Blacks in one place. Coming to school every day and sharing their reflected light was a learning experience that reinforced the classroom lessons.

A self-perpetuating mythology would develop later around inner-city Black schools. Many people, including many educators, would buy into the dumb idea that poor Black students can't and won't learn. Our teachers didn't believe that. They believed we could do anything we wanted to do, and they challenged us to reach for the stars.

Mary J. Herrick, our civics teacher, was one of the most unforgettable persons I've known. She was White, but she was so sincere and spoke with so much conviction that she became a legend in Black Chicago. She took us on field trips to downtown Chicago and told us what was happening in Washington and London. She also invited us into her home for tea—she was the first White person to invite me into her home on a social basis.

For the first time I learned something about Africa. The true story was not in the books, but Mary J. Herrick taught it. She told us we were descendants of an ancient people who created major civilizations in Africa and challenged us to prepare ourselves for the next lap of a great race.

There's nothing wrong with public education that more resources, more love, more C. S. Johnsons and Mary Herricks can't cure. Our most important task is to duplicate the nurturing, transforming environment that made it possible for unsung and underpaid teachers and administrators, Black and White, to perform the educational miracles of yesterday.

Mary Herrick taught as if her life—and our lives—depended on it. She was the first White person I'd met who was completely free of racial prejudice.

Wendell Phillips High School later burned, and the student body was transferred to a newly constructed building, which was named later for the Black father of Chicago, Jean Baptiste Pointe du Sable. Among my classmates at both institutions was Nathaniel Cole, the stick-thin son of the Reverend Edward Cole, who couldn't sing but achieved local fame as the piano player at the "Spotlight" dances at the Warwick Hall of Forty-third Street. They were called "Spotlight" dances because it was the custom to turn off the lights and shine spotlights on various couples to see if they were dancing too close.

Large crowds flocked to these dances. Not, however, to listen to pianist Cole, who went on to attract larger crowds as Nat King Cole. Nobody, not even Nat, knew he could sing then. This hidden talent emerged one night on the West Coast when his singer didn't show up and the nightclub owner demanded a song.

7
The Boy in the Mirror

If the worst thing in the world is to be poor in a rich country, as W. E. B. DuBois said, the next worst thing is to be the poorest person in a poor country.

Most of my classmates were poor, but I was poorer than most. Since there was no money for buses, I walked to school, even in the bitter-cold months. And I wore homemade suits and pants.

As if that wasn't enough, I was shy, insecure, inarticulate, and I spoke in a thick down-home country accent. How could any self-respecting student comic resist such a target? They came from all over, from the ninth grade and the tenth grade and the twelfth grade, to poke fun at the country boy from Arkansas. They laughed at my "mammy-made" clothes. They laughed at my accent. You know the result.

If your classmates laugh every time you stand up to recite, if they follow you, shouting, "Look at that bowlegged boy in his mammy-made clothes"—if this happens every day and you have no friends or money and are alone in a strange city, you begin to feel put upon.

I remember running home crying and telling my mother, who quickly and quietly resolved one aspect of the problem. She was working then for a woman whose husband was about my size, and she persuaded the couple to give us some old suits. Almost overnight I became one of the best-dressed students at the old and the new Wendell Phillips.

I resented the way I was treated by some students, and I decided to retaliate the only way I knew how—by beating them in class and in extracurricular activities. From the time I entered Wendell Phillips in 1933 until I graduated from DuSable in 1936, I studied harder, partly because I didn't have enough money to take girls out, and partly because I wanted to even the score. I also read self-improvement books by Dale Carnegie and others.

Faith, self-confidence, and a positive mental attitude: these three were the basic messages of the self-help books that changed my life.

Most of these books listed one-two-three practical steps for improving personal effectiveness. One step was to practice conversations and selling approaches in private before trying them out in public.

I started practicing speeches and approaches to girls before the mirror at home. Everybody was out working, and I could talk as loud and as long as I wanted to. Day in and day out, I alternately lectured and talked sweet to that mirror. Then I went to school and forced myself to stand up and speak in class. They laughed at first, but they soon started applauding— because I was making sense and because I was a good speaker. This experience taught me that one of the sweetest emotions in the world is watching scorn turn into admiration and awe.

I learned something else that I've never forgotten: *there is no defense against an excellence that speaks to a real need.*

This brings us back, at a new and different level, to the advantage of the disadvantage. If I had been rich with a lot of friends, I wouldn't be where I am today. It's not satisfaction but dissatisfaction that drives people to the heights. I was goaded, I was driven to success by the whip of social disapproval.

Throughout the thirties and on into the forties, I read and reread books on self-improvement, success, and selling. One of my favorites was *Think and Grow Rich.* Another was Dale Carnegie's *How to Win Friends and Influence People.*

Perhaps the most important lesson I learned from these books was "other-focusing." We live, all of us, too close to ourselves. And all of us need to focus more on what others want rather than on what we want.

If there's one thing that life teaches us, it's that people everywhere act to preserve or advance their own interests. And if you want people to satisfy a need that is vital to *your* self-interest, you've got to study them and figure out what *they* want. You can't be indifferent to them. Nor can you challenge everything they say and do. Not if you want them to help you.

If that's your goal—and half the battle in winning friends and influencing people is defining your goal and the other person's goal—you've got to study people and make it to *their* self-interest to advance *your* self-interest.

I read all the self-help books I could find. I also read the great classics of Black history and literature, including Booker T. Washington's autobiography, *Up From Slavery*, W. E. B. DuBois's essays, and the poetry of Langston Hughes.

Vivian Harsh, the librarian at the Forth-eighth Street branch of the Chicago Public Library, had one of the major collections of books on the Black experience. I used to hang out in the branch, reading books on Frederick Douglass and other Blacks who had succeeded against the odds.

Chicago was at the center of the dominant currents of the age—Ethiopia's struggle against Italy, the "Don't Buy Where You Can't Work" movement, the Scottsboro Campaign. These issues were discussed at public forums in Washington Park and in city churches by the leading Black personalities of the day. These forums were free, and I took advantage of an urban environment that was itself a public education.

The months and years of reading and listening and practicing paid off. When the students met to organize the junior class, the sponsoring teacher asked if anyone had anything to say. No one moved. No one said a word.

After a long and uncomfortable pause, I got up and expressed appreciation to the sponsor for giving us an opportunity to organize. I said we were happy to be in this new school and that we would work hard to justify the confidence that the teachers had placed in us.

This was not, all things considered, a very original presentation, but my fellow students were evidently pleased, for I was immediately and unanimously elected junior class president. I was also editor-in-chief of the *Phillipsite*, presiding officer of the student council, leader of the student forum and the French Club.

When I graduated, the yearbook said Johnny Johnson had "participated in so many activities that the teachers will have to find four or five other students to fill his place."

The one activity I shunned was sports. I was so involved in trying to think my way out of poverty I didn't even take gym.

For a long time, I thought I was peculiar. Then one day I read a story in *Fortune* magazine about Stanley Burnet Resor, the head of J. Walter Thompson advertising agency. The story said "his food and drink, his unremitting daily task, and the substance of his dreams is advertising. He has no hobbies, plays no games."

I put the magazine down with a sigh of relief. At last, I said, I've found a guy like me. For I have no hobbies and play no games, and the food and drink of my life is trying to succeed.

Although I operate in a world that is made up of part-time golfers and sportsmen, success is still my hobby. I had an amusing encounter with an industrialist who assumed that I was the token Black on the board and offered unsolicited advice on how to make it in corporate America.

"Do you play golf?" he asked. I said no. He said, "Johnson, you're never going to get anywhere in this world until you learn how to play golf."

I had no interest, then or now, in hitting little white balls, but like all teenagers, I had a passionate interest in the opposite sex. But that was one game that couldn't be played without adequate wherewithal. Although my approach, honed to a fine edge by practice in front of a mirror, was pretty good, my social life was limited by lack of money to take young ladies to the Regal and other citadels of entertainment.

I had a crush on one young lady who lived within walking distance of the Regal—because of my poverty I could only fall in love with girls who didn't require carfare to get to the Regal. She agreed one day to go to the show with me and then decided at the last moment to go for a ride with a former classmate who'd dropped out of school to work at the post office.

Meanwhile, I continued my feverish and largely unsuccessful effort to find pretty and persuadable young girls who lived within walking distance of the show.

8
My Days on Welfare

In late 1933, mother, Beulah, and I moved to an apartment at 5412 South Parkway, a large structure built around a courtyard. We had four rooms, a bedroom, living room, kitchen, and dining room, and we paid thirty-five dollars a month.

Beulah and mother slept in the bedroom, and I slept on a rollaway bed in the dining room. For twenty-three years, I slept on couches and rollaway beds. In fact, I never had a bedroom of my own until I got married.

Before long, my stepfather decided to move to Chicago. As soon as he arrived, the crazy quilt of our lives came apart at the seams, and the dire predictions he'd made in Arkansas came true.

My stepfather arrived at the height of the Depression and couldn't find a job anywhere. Then, in rapid-fire order, my mother lost her job as a domestic and Beulah lost her job in the garment industry. Complicating things even more, Beulah joined the Father Divine Movement and went through a painful conversion crisis.

This required some fast footwork, and we danced to the music of the times, renting out our only bedroom and making other economies. We rented the bedroom for five dollars a week. This provided twenty of the thirty-five dollars we needed for the monthly rent. Somehow, we managed to scrounge up the additional fifteen dollars each month.

My mother and stepfather slept in the dining room. I slept on a couch in the living room. Despite the desperation of the period, we were never hungry. We ate more neck bones than we wanted. We ate more leftovers than we wanted. But there was always something to eat.

My mother turned out to be an economic magician who always came up with money from somewhere at hole-card time. Always, when it seemed that there was no way out, she would look in a shoe box or a cookie jar or behind the canned goods and say, "Well, I was putting this aside for a rainy day...." Perhaps the most important lesson I learned from her is that life is so uncertain that you should always have something hidden under a cookie jar that you can use for survival.

But the economic crisis of the thirties was bigger than private cookie jars. And we were forced, like millions of other Americans, to apply for welfare, or relief, as it was known then. Our application was rejected on the grounds that we hadn't lived in Chicago long enough. My mother sat down, in one of the great inspirations in her life, and wrote a letter to the president of the United States. She told President Roosevelt that she and her husband couldn't find work, that she had a son to support and would he please tell the local authorities to accept us.

One of President Roosevelt's secrets of success was that he answered letters. President Roosevelt probably didn't see my mother's letter, but it found its way to Chicago and the local bureaucrats put us on relief.

My mother, who was, like almost all Blacks, a Republican, became an instant Democrat. From that day forward, she was a devoted supporter of Roosevelt and his works. She believed until her death that he had personally answered her letter.

From late 1934 until 1936, we were on relief. In these years, welfare came not in monthly checks but in monthly visits by government trucks. On the first days of the month, the big government trucks would roar through the South Side, like invading convoys, dropping off salt pork, beans, peas, and other commodities.

What I remember most about my days on welfare was the shame. I used to sit on a stoop with a group of young men and watch the welfare trucks cruising the neighborhood. The trucks would drive up to my house, and someone would say, "They're going to *your* house." And I would say, "That's not my house." The truck would drive up to someone else's house, and he would say, "That's not my house." We knew the trucks were going to our houses; we were just too ashamed to admit it.

The problem, I think, is the purpose of welfare and the

organization of the welfare system. The goal must always be to get *off* welfare, and we got off as soon as we could.

We got off the welfare rolls two years later when my stepfather got a WPA job, and I got a job with a division of the National Youth Administration, two of the New Deal programs intended to battle the Depression.

We need to think deeply about these programs that saved the American economic system, and about what John F. Kennedy meant when he said, "If a free society cannot help the many who are poor, it cannot save the few who are rich."

Because we received help at a critical moment in our lives and because we never lost the will to end dependence on welfare, we broke free and began the slow rise to that economic emancipation without which political emancipation is a mere mockery. But something of the shame and terror of those days remains with me to this day. If I don't feel like getting up in the morning, all I do to motivate myself is to recall the government truck stopping in front of my house—and I jump up and go to work.

9
The Birth of
John Harold Johnson

Still in high school, I was organizing forums and even a mimeographed magazine (*Afri-American Youth*) for the National Youth Administration.

I was also involved in the planning for the DuSable High School commencement. The commencement was held on Thursday, June 11, 1936, and I was the only student speaker. On Saturday, June 6, I received my first press notice in the *Chicago Defender*, which said I would speak on the subject "Builders of a New World."

"Builders of a New World": I don't know whether I changed my mind or whether this was only a part of my title. At any rate, I spoke on the subject "The Task That Lies Before Us." The title provocatively emphasized the task, not the tasks. What precisely was this task? The task, I said, was excellence linked to service. It was a speech I could and probably will give tomorrow. And I'm pleased to find myself in agreement with the young John H. Johnson.

This commencement also marked the birth of John H. Johnson. My official name was Johnny Johnson and I fully intended to graduate that way. But Miss Herrick, the sensitive civics teacher, pulled me aside and said, "Johnny, you're about to graduate. You're a big boy now. Shouldn't you be John?"

I thought about it for a moment and said yes. She then said, "Perhaps you ought to have a middle name."

I picked a name out of the air, and Johnny Johnson became John Harold Johnson.

By whatever name, I was confused and crestfallen. I'd just graduated with a fistful of honors and a scholarship to the University of Chicago, but the scholarship only paid two hundred dollars, and I had two months to get or borrow enough money to finance a year's study at Chicago or some other institution of higher learning.

This problem seemed to be beyond my control, but I've

learned over the years that the best way to deal with an insoluble problem is to get up on the balls of your feet and keep moving, like a good boxer. While you're moving, something might hit you, or you might hit something or someone. I kept moving and walked—was it an accident or was it fate?—into the turning point of my life.

The moment occurred at a routine Urban League luncheon for outstanding high school students. The main speaker was one of my heroes, a legendary business leader named Harry H. Pace. He was president of Supreme Liberty Life Insurance Company, the biggest Black business in the North and in Chicago. Pace spoke brilliantly, calling for work, service, struggle, and excellence.

When he finished, I was one of the first students to reach him. I was a long way now from the insecure and inarticulate student who'd arrived in Chicago, a bare three years before, with a cardboard suitcase and brown paper bag. Because of Dale Carnegie and all those hours in front of the mirror, I could express myself, and I had no difficulty in telling Pace how much I appreciated his remarks. He returned the compliment, saying he'd heard good reports about my high school record.

"What do you plan to do now?" he asked.

"I want to go to college," I said, "but I don't have enough money."

"Have you thought about working part-time and studying part-time?"

I said I had thought of nothing else but that I couldn't find a part-time or a full-time job. He paused for a moment—and my life changed forever.

"I'm going away on vacation," he said, "but I'll be back in September. See me on the first working day in September, and I'll find something for you to do."

Somebody asked me once what I would change if I could live my life over again. I replied that I wouldn't change anything. So many things happened along the way, maybe by accident, maybe by Providence, that I would be afraid to change any of the events that led to the meeting with Harry H. Pace and the big ebony road that changed and defined my life.

10
Supreme Life
and the Double-Duty Dollar

I walked into the headquarters of Supreme Liberty Life Insurance Company on Tuesday, September 1, 1936, and asked for President and CEO Harry H. Pace.

"The president," I said, "is expecting me."

This was a bold gambit for an eighteen-year-old youth, and it marked the beginning of my third life, following the first fifteen years in Arkansas City and the dramatic change after the escape to Chicago.

President Pace wasn't expecting me, but he'd told me to report on this day. And I spent an uncomfortable fifteen minutes wondering whether he would remember our conversation and his promise to give me a job.

While waiting, I looked around and noticed a strange phenomenon.

Right before my eyes, men and women, *good-looking, well-dressed* men and women, were scurrying from office to office with stacks of papers and fat files.

What was going on here?

I'd seen photographs and movies of White men and women running around like this and making deals in the offices of the Rockefellers and Morgans. But the men and women before me were Black, like me. And they were moving paper and talking big money talk just like White folk.

This was a new thing, and I sat up and paid attention.

Until that moment, the height and color of my dream had been set by the ceiling and color of the Black preachers, teachers, and lawyers I'd seen. I'd heard about Black corporations, but I'd never examined one up close. Now, suddenly, I was surrounded by Black clerks, salesmen, and money managers. And just like that—click, click, click, click, CLICK!—lights went on in my mind and my life.

In that light, with mounting excitement, I examined this new card that life had put into my hands.

I knew from my research—I was only eighteen years old, but I already knew that you never go into a man's office unless you know more about him, about his background, his interests, hobbies, loves, than he knows about you—that Supreme Liberty (now Supreme Life) was the product of the 1929 merger of three Black companies.

This was one of the first major mergers in American business history, and it was at that time the biggest financial deal ever negotiated by all-Black businesses.

The merger was engineered by a group of brilliant men, notably Pace, who became president and CEO; Earl B. Dickerson, who became general counsel, and Truman K. Gibson, who became chairman and received the Harmon Award for his role in the negotiations.

The new president, Harry Herbert Pace, was one of the most interesting and enigmatic figures in the history of Black America. He had more sides, in fact, than a geodesic dome. He was a scholar, lawyer, author, entrepreneur, entertainment impresario, and philosopher. He was also an activist who played a major role in many of the big social and economic movements of the first decades of the century.

He was a master of networking who carried the art of mentoring to new heights. Pace discovered and gave that first crucial helping hand to more Black artists and leaders than any other American. He was the first person to hire bandleader Fletcher Henderson and actresses Isabelle Washington and Freddie Washington. He discovered Ethel Waters and Trixie Smith and was the first person to attract national attention to the work of W. C. Handy.

A graduate of Atlanta University and the Chicago Law School, a former teacher of Latin and Greek, Pace had a genius for new trends and new talent. Walter White, the longtime leader of the NAACP, got his start as a Pace office boy, and it was Pace who recommended him to the NAACP hierarchy. Paul Robeson sold records in Pace's music shop while he was a law student at Columbia University.

Pace was only fifty-two on the day I reported for work, but

he had served as president and CEO of several businesses, including the New York-based Pace and Handy Music Company and Black Swan Phonograph Company. Black Swan, a forerunner of Motown, tried to control the millions flowing from the songs and rhythms of Black America.

This was the first major Black-owned recording company, and it led to the Beatles and the Grammies.

This was the man, brilliant, bold, far-seeing, who welcomed me on September 1, 1936, and assigned me to an empty desk outside his door. I learned later that he really didn't have anything for me to do. He was just a considerate man who took great pride in recognizing youths he considered talented and promising.

After sitting at this desk for three or four months without being called on to do anything substantial, I decided one day to sneak out and get a soda at a nearby drugstore. At that precise moment, Pace did something he'd never done before: he called and asked me to come into his office.

When I got back, he said, "Young man, one thing you've got to learn. I'm paying you to sit at your desk, and you should stay there even if I *never* call you." From then on, I stayed at the desk, whether I was called or not, and gradually the job assumed more importance.

I received twenty-five dollars a month and worked part-time at Supreme while attending the University of Chicago part-time. I intended at that time to pursue a law degree, but the Supreme Liberty curriculum was so exciting that I dropped out of the university and devoted myself full-time to my studies at Supreme.

I wouldn't recommend this approach today. A college degree is a basic necessity in the technocratic environment as we head into a new century. A student who drops out of college in this environment drops out of the race for personal fulfillment and economic security.

The situation was different when I started work at Supreme. At that point, in the depth of the Depression, the key factor was a job, not a degree. I knew several well-educated

Blacks, lawyers, doctors, and dentists, who were working at the post office. Under these circumstances, it was not at all surprising that I seized the white-collar opportunity that Supreme provided.

The company had succeeded in building a strong presence in a field where the high Black mortality rate had frightened off White investors. It was so successful in this effort that it survived the Depression and continued to make loans to Black property owners when White banks and realtors were routinely turning down Black applicants.

Supreme survived, because it was superior in dealing with the challenges of an unfavorable business environment. When Supreme and other Black-owned institutions changed that environment and created a large and prosperous middle class, White corporations reevaluated the Black consumer market.

Supreme was a sound business, and it was a sound *Black* business. It emphasized the double-duty dollar, telling Blacks that a dollar invested in Supreme provided insurance protection *and* employment for Black men and women.

"Spend Your Money Where You Can Work." This was the characteristic theme of company agents.

What this meant on a practical level was that Supreme, like other Black businesses, was *more* than a business. It was a statement, a petition, a demonstration, and an argument. That's what Booker T. Washington meant when he said:

"One farm bought, one house built...one man who is the largest tax-payer or has the largest bank account, one school or church maintained, one factory running successfully...one patient cured by a Negro doctor, one sermon well preached, one office well filled—these will tell more in our favor than all the abstract eloquence that can be summoned to plead our cause."

This was the history, and the hope, of the double-duty dollar that shaped my business horizon. I had been looking for this fulcrum all my life, without knowing what I was looking for, and without even knowing that I was looking. Now that I'd found Supreme, I threw myself on it as a drowning man throws himself on a plank, not because it was better than a boat but because it was the only boat I had.

My brother-in-law, the late Dr. William Walker, an eminent surgeon, told me once that he envied businessmen because they, unlike doctors and other professionals, can make money even when they're not working.

"Brother Johnny," he said, "I only make money when I'm working on a patient. But you make money even when you're asleep. Even while we're sitting here talking at one o'clock in the morning, people somewhere are buying your magazines and products and making money for you."

That's part of the lure of business, but it's only a part. For after the first million or two, money is only a means of measuring and keeping count. What has fascinated me, then and now, has been the electricity of making a deal, the challenge of managing the human elements, and the adrenaline-flowing gamble of keeping nine or ten balls in the air and bringing them down safely and walking away with a flair.

It was the dare, it was the gamble, it was the *deal* that captivated me. I was on the bottom rung at Supreme, but coming to work and watching Pace and his associates play with millions gave me a physical thrill.

Another element in this equation was the magic of journalism. For me, as well as for Pace, journalism was a skyscraper value precisely because it combined the ultimate business challenge with the ultimate social challenge. A magazine—and we were both interested in magazines—could not survive if it wasn't based on sound business principles. But sound business principles alone would not ensure its survival. That was the dilemma, and nobody in Black America had solved it.

Since the founding of *The Mirror of Liberty* in 1838, there had been scores of Black magazines. But they died, one after another, of terminal cash flow. Despite this history, the idea lived on and bewitched several men. Among them, Harry Pace, who was a frustrated journalist until the day he died.

It was this passion that provided my first opening. I was assigned to the company's monthly newspaper, *The Guardian*, first as assistant to the editor, who was, of course, Harry H. Pace.

After three or four months, I was named assistant editor. In 1939 I was promoted to editor.

This was a strategic post for an ambitious young man, and I made the most of it to study people, success, and power. I was guided by more than academic curiosity. I had six bosses, and my survival depended on a close understanding of the six members on the company executive committee. To give you an idea of the importance and the delicacy of this task, I used a ruler to make sure that I gave each of the six men the same amount of space in each edition of the monthly company newspaper.

I learned a lot from these men. I drove President Pace to the bank almost every day, and I used the opportunity to ask questions about business, life, success, and Black America. Not a week goes by that I don't recall and use some lesson that I learned from him and other Supreme executives.

Among other things, I learned how to ration my time and focus my activities. As a result, I'm never thrown off stride by people who barge in without an appointment. I simply tell these interlopers that I'm sorry that I can't see them or listen to their pleas, but that I had planned my day without knowing that they were going to call or come by.

I also learned how to size up a situation and determine if it advanced my interests. This was perhaps the most important lesson of all, for our destiny is, in large part, in our own hands. We are exposed daily to situations and people who can drive us up the wall *if we let them.* Most of these people and situations have little or no bearing on our life goals and can be ignored or relegated to the margins.

Even as a young man, I governed my life by this principle. If a situation was in line with what I wanted personally, I focused all my energies on that one point. While I was dealing with that point, I dealt with it completely, to the exclusion of everything else. If, on the other hand, it wasn't what I wanted, I simply rejected it, without wasting time, emotion, or energy.

In addition to concrete lessons, I was exposed to "live" cases that forced me to draw my own conclusions. I learned, for example, that circumstances, people, and even the temperature can alter cases and that a rule that produces a stunning success on Monday will wreak havoc if applied rigidly on Tuesday.

This means that business, for all its reliance on business machines and numbers, is an art, not a science. It means also that business schools have limits. For the many important things an executive needs to know can't be taught.

All this was fascinating, and I drifted further and further away from my educational goals. I kept telling myself that I would go back at some point and finish my college studies, but as I moved up the ladder, I became more and more involved in company affairs.

I attended company conventions and business conferences, and went out into the field and sold insurance to get a better understanding of the industry. Supreme by now was my whole life. I could hardly wait to get to the Thirty-fifth and South Parkway office in the morning.

Part of Supreme's fascination was that it was a world that contained everything and reached out to everything in Black Chicago. All of the gossip, all of the power plays and social maneuvers came, sooner or later, to the crossroads at Thirty-fifth and South Parkway. Practically every major event in Black Chicago between 1936 and 1942 was planned, organized, or financed by people who orbited around the Supreme sun.

11
Wedding in Selma

By the end of the thirties, I was making enough money—fifty dollars a week from Supreme Liberty and another fifty dollars from my political secretary's post—to buy my first car, a light brown 1940 Chevrolet. No purchase since—neither my first Cadillac nor my first Rolls-Royce— has given me more undiluted pleasure.

In the same year, I met a pretty young woman who later became my wife. Her name was Eunice Walker, and she was a Talladega College student vacationing in Chicago.

We met by accident one night at a dance at Bacon's Casino at Forty-ninth Street and Wabash. I went to the dance with another young woman, and she went to the dance with another young man. We were introduced by mutual friends, and sparks began to fly. After graduating from Talladega, she got a master's degree in social work from Chicago's Loyola University.

I found out later that she was the daughter of one of the first Black families of the South. Her father, Nathaniel D. Walker, was a physician in Selma, Alabama. Her maternal grandfather, Dr. William H. McAlpine, was one of the founders of Selma University and the National Baptist Convention.

I was not, to put it mildly, one of the great catches of 1940. People used to tell Eunice that she was wasting her time keeping company with a young man of doubtful background who was not among the young Black professionals who were most likely to succeed.

What impressed me about Eunice in comparison with the other young women I had known is that our relationship was not just a romance—it was a meeting of the minds. She was interesting and interested in what was going on in the world. She was a good listener, sympathetic to my ambitions. She made me feel that maybe I would be somebody one day.

After dating for a year, we were married in Selma, Alabama, on June 21, 1941.

Shortly before the wedding, I bought my second car, a red Studebaker. Eunice took the train to Selma, and I drove down. A trip through the South in those days for a Black man with a red car and Illinois license plates was a daring experience, but fate was with us and we made it to Selma for the wedding.

There was not enough money for a traditional trip. We honeymooned by driving back to Chicago, and shortly afterward moved into a three-room apartment.

Before the year was out, bombs exploded in Pearl Harbor. We were in World War II.

I registered for the draft. At that time, the board held a lottery of the 4,000 registrants and I was 3990-something. This meant that I wasn't going to be called right away.

12
Millions Made With a $500 Loan

At about this time, Harry Pace gave me an assignment that changed my life. He said he wanted me to read magazines and newspapers and prepare a digest of what was happening in the Black world.

We met at least once a week, usually on Monday, and I gave him a briefing so he could talk intelligently about race relations to people who came to his office.

It would have been possible in contemporary America—largely because of the Civil Rights Movement and *Negro Digest* and *Jet* and *Ebony*—for him to get some of this information in White media, but in that period there was an almost total White-out on positive Black news in White-oriented media.

There was an unwritten rule in the South in this period that a Black's picture could not appear in the press unless in connection with a crime. There was no consistent coverage of the human dimensions of Black Americans in northern newspapers and magazines. It's hard to make people realize this, but Blacks didn't get married on the society pages of major American dailies until the late sixties.

The items I gathered for Pace from the Negro press and isolated reports in the White press made me one of the most knowledgeable persons in Black Chicago. I started telling my friends about the amazing things I'd read. And I was usually the center of attention at social gatherings where, like some traveling circuit rider, I gave a digest of Negro news or a Negro digest. The response was almost always the same: "Where can I find that article?" Some people said they would pay me if I would let them know where this or that article appeared.

The next step was so obvious that I'm ashamed to say that I didn't immediately recognize it. I'd been riding the social circuit for several weeks, reciting my stories of Black achievement and aspiration, before it occurred to me that I was looking at a black gold mine. And that I could be successful on a limited scale with a Negro digest which would pass on to the public the material I'd been digesting for Pace.

The problem here was not my density but a general climate of doubt surrounding Black publications. Most people had seen *Reader's Digest* and *Time*, but nobody had seen a successful Black commercial magazine. And nobody was willing to risk a penny on a twenty-four-year-old insurance worker and what people told him at cocktail parties.

That's been the story of my life. At every critical turning point in my life, people, Black and White, always told me no at first. And I almost always had to turn the nos into yeses.

For almost two months, week after week, I went from office to office in Black Chicago and was told no and hell no. I remember going to New York to get the blessings of Roy Wilkins, the editor of the most successful Black magazine, *The Crisis*, the noncommercial house organ of the NAACP.

Roy listened to my story and said, "Save your money, young man. Save your energy. Save yourself a lot of disappointment." Roy went on to become NAACP executive director, and one of the sweet moments of my life was when he called me and said, "Johnny, you know, I think I gave you some bad advice." He returned to the same theme in his autobiography, *Standing Fast*.

"One day in the early forties," he wrote, "a bright and eager young man named John Johnson came to the office to talk to me about an idea he had for starting a new magazine, a pocket-sized publication that would summarize newspaper and magazine articles about Negro life. I knew the almost continuous financial difficulties *The Crisis* had, and I told him that in my opinion the time was not right to venture into the field. Fortunately, Johnson ignored me...."

I got bad advice from a lot of people who also gave themselves bad advice. There are at least two people who would be multimillionaires today if they had invested the $1,000 I was asking forty-seven years ago. I will forever be grateful to them. If they'd invested back then, I wouldn't be the sole owner of

Johnson Publishing Company today.

When I had exhausted every avenue of support, I returned to Johnson Rule No. 1—What can you do by yourself, with what you have, to get what you want?—and I made some interesting discoveries. As the low man in the Supreme power structure, I had accumulated some small tasks that I hated. For example, I ran the Speedaumat, an addressing machine which kept the names and addresses of the twenty thousand people who paid their insurance premiums quarterly, semiannually, or annually.

I looked at the mailing list. I looked at the Speedaumat. And an idea—wild, unbelievable, but definitely possible—grew in my mind. Why not send a letter to every person on the list, asking for a two-dollar prepaid subscription to a new Black magazine? If I got a 30 percent response ($12,000) or even a 15 percent response ($6,000), I would have the money to publish the first issue of the magazine. I discussed the idea with Pace, who said I could use the names and the machine.

"Since you are running the machine anyway," he said, "there's no reason why you can't use it to mail the letters."

There's a lesson in this incident. There are so many twists and turns in a life that you never know where a job, however small, will lead you. It's in your best interest, then, to do every task assigned you well, for you never know when these skills can be utilized later.

Although I resented some of the little things I was doing, one of them—running the Speedaumat machine—was the key to the *Negro Digest* sweepstakes.

I had the twenty thousand names, I knew how to run the machine, and I had permission to use the company's clear stationery. There was only one more hurdle: I needed $500 to buy stamps.

If you've ever been in this situation, you know how I felt. I was so close to victory that I could taste it, and yet I was so far away. Five hundred dollars. That was a lot of money in 1942. Where could I get $500?

I must have been desperate, for I did something that was

unheard-of in those days. I went to the First National Bank of Chicago and asked for a $500 loan to start a business. I'm one of First National's premium customers today—but the assistant to the assistant that I managed to see in 1942 laughed in my face.

"Boy," he said, "we don't make any loans to colored people."

I felt a flash of anger, but the self-help books I'd been reading said don't get mad, get smart. I got smart and looked the assistant to the assistant in the eye and said, "Who in this town will loan money to a colored person?"

"The only place I know," he answered looking at me with new interest, "is the Citizens Loan Corporation at Sixty-third and Cottage Grove."

I asked if he knew anyone at Citizens, and he gave me a name.

"Can I tell him that you referred me?"

He looked at me now as if seeing me for the first time and said, "Of course."

The man at the loan company said, "Yes we'll give you a loan but only if you have collateral."

"What do you mean by collateral?" I asked.

He said a house that you can mortgage or new furniture or some tangible asset that you can pledge as a guarantee that you'll repay the loan can be collateral.

I didn't have a house to mortgage, but my mother had managed with my help to buy some new furniture. I asked her to let me use it as collateral for a $500 loan. For the first time in all the years I'd known her, she frowned and balked. It had taken her a long time to pay for the furniture. She was proud of it. And she didn't intend to lose it. I pleaded and she said, "I'll just have to consult the Lord about this. It's not a decision I can make by myself."

Every day, for almost a week, I'd come home and check with my mother to see if the Lord had said anything, and she'd say, "No, I'm still praying."

I said, "Maybe I'd better pray with you."

For three or four days, we prayed together and cried together. Finally, she said, "I think the Lord wants me to do it." She gave me the paid-up document, and I took it to the guy at the loan company and was issued a check for $500.

I had already drafted the letter—I never doubted for one moment that the Lord would say the word—which was based on the most important axiom of salesmanship: *Ask not what you want but what the customer or the potential customer wants.* This was my whole selling campaign for *Negro Digest.* It is an elementary rule violated daily by beginners and seasoned salesmen who barge into offices and make sales pitches based on what they need and want. The world doesn't care about what you need or want. What the world wants to know is what you can do for others.

Perhaps the biggest violators of this rule are job applicants who tell you how much they need a job and how much it would mean to them. That's the wrong approach. The correct approach is to tell the customer or potential employer what you can do to advance his interest. The job applicant who studies a company and its needs and tells the interviewer what he or she can do for the company is more than halfway home.

The important point is that your sales pitch should be based not on your self-interest but on their self-interest and on what they want most. Not, mind you, on what they say they want but on what they *really* want.

This rule has served me well over the years. The only way I got to where I am today was by persuading thousands of Blacks and Whites, some of whom were very prejudiced, that the only way they could get what they wanted was by helping me get what I wanted.

This, then, was the situation.

I was writing a letter to twenty thousand Black Americans in 1942. What did they want? The answer was obvious. They wanted what everybody else wanted. They wanted recognition, the good life, and, in Aretha Franklin's word, r-e-s-p-e-c-t.

Respect.

For more than one hundred years, that had been the cry of

the Black soul. One hundred years of "boy" and "girl" and "George" and "Mary" and "nigger" had created an almost inexhaustible thirst for recognition and respect.

In 1942, Black men and women were struggling all over America for the right to be called "Mr." and "Mrs." In that year, we couldn't try on hats in department stores in Baltimore, and we couldn't try on shoes and dresses in Atlanta. We couldn't live in hotels in downtown Chicago then, and the only public place a Black could get a meal in the downtown section of the nation's capital was the railroad station.

It was in this world that *Negro Digest* was conceived. It was a world where the primary need, almost as demanding as oxygen, was recognition and respect.

I wanted the letter to say to Blacks that I intended to put out a magazine that would increase their respect and add to their knowledge and understanding. I still remember every word and comma of the letter I wrote:

> Dear Mr. Brown:
> A good friend of yours told me about you. He told me that you are a person who likes to keep abreast of local and national events. He said you are the kind of person who will be interested in a magazine that will help you become more knowledgeable about your own people and about what they are doing to win greater recognition for you and other members of our race. Because of your position in the community and the recommendation I received, I would like to offer you a reduced rate on the magazine *Negro Digest*, which will be published in the next thirty days. Magazine subscriptions will sell for $3.00 a year, but in view of the recommendation we are offering a subscription to you for $2.00, if you send your check or money order by September 30.

Before sending this letter, I took the precaution of securing my first office and mailing address. One of my supervisors, Earl Dickerson, had a private law office and a law library in a private section of the Supreme building. I asked if I could use a corner of the law library, which contained old books and was seldom used. He said okay, and I moved a desk into the corner of the office, which was on the second floor of the Supreme building but had another entrance and another address, 3507 South Parkway.

This was the first address of what was then called Negro Digest Publishing Company. From June to November, I worked downstairs in the insurance company in the day and climbed the stairs at night to work on the magazine. One day in the summer of 1942 a man came and painted letters on the frosty glass door—Negro Digest Publishing Company—and every letter was music to my soul.

It was from this office that I sent letters to twenty thousand persons asking for prepublication subscriptions. Three thousand persons—an unusually high percentage—responded, sending $6,000.

While all this was going on, I drafted and sent out letters asking for the right to publish certain stories and articles that had appeared in Black newspapers and White magazines and periodicals. My wife, who was a social worker by day, helped at night, stuffing envelopes and assisting in editorial and circulation tasks. So did Jay Jackson, a brilliant artist and cartoonist who worked for the *Chicago Defender*, and Ben Burns, a White free-lance writer I'd met when we both worked on Earl Dickerson's campaign.

By October, there was only one remaining hurdle: finding a printing press and persuading the owner of the press to extend credit until the magazines were printed and sold. Here, once again, Supreme came to the rescue. One of my duties at Supreme was running the multilith machine and dealing with Progress Printing Company, which printed material for the insurance company. When I went to the printer's office and told him that "we" were thinking about publishing a magazine, he assumed that I was talking about the insurance company, when I was really talking about myself. Since he assumed that the magazine was either owned or backed by the insurance company, he started working without worrying about how I was going to pay him.

By these methods and others, I maneuvered, negotiated, pleaded, begged, screamed, shouted, cursed, prayed my way to the watershed day of Sunday, November 1, 1942.

The following events occurred on that day:

A small force of U.S. Marines crossed the Mataniko River on the western frontier of Guadalcanal and attacked the Japanese, who were reported to be retreating slowly.

At Stalingrad, Russian forces repulsed attacks by the Nazis.

The U.S. government took over all short-wave broadcast stations.

Senator Elbert D. Thomas, Democrat, Utah, spoke at a New York rally commemorating the twenty-fifth anniversary of the Balfour Declaration and called for the immediate establishment of a Jewish national home in Palestine.

The Chicago Bears football team defeated Detroit by a score of 16 to 0.

A new magazine, *Negro Digest*, "a magazine of Negro comment," was published officially for the first time.

All of these events, with the exception of the debut of *Negro Digest*, were noted by the White press. *Negro Digest* came into the world unheralded and unnoticed, except by the publisher, who was born again that day.

Before the week was out, there were scattered comments in the Black press. On November 7, the *Pittsburgh Courier* printed a story on the new magazine, under the heading "New Negro Digest Answering Demands."

The lead paragraph said: "Should Negroes care who wins the war? Is the Negro demand for full equality sabotaging the war effort? These questions, along with many other vital ones, are answered in the November issue of NegroDigest... published this week in Chicago." The paper said managing editor John H. Johnson was a native of Arkansas who has been "for the past several years...director of publicity for the Supreme Liberty Life Insurance Company."

When I held the first copy of the magazine in my hand, I

had a feeling of relief, exhilaration, and fear. I hadn't realized the true potential of the magazine until that moment, and I was overwhelmed by the idea that the life and death of this sixty-eight-page baby was in my hands.

The two-color cover (red and blue) of the 7½ by 5 inch magazine carried the title and explanation, "A Magazine of Negro Comment," and a list of the articles and features. There were contributions by Carl Sandburg, Walter White, John P. Lewis, Marquis W. Childs, Langston Hughes, Rabbi Harry Essrig and Bishop Bernard Sheil. This was not a bad group of people to hang out with. And the typography and layout emphasized excellence and quality. There was only one name on the masthead, "Managing Editor: John H. Johnson."

Why was this magazine published? What did it intend to do and say? The opening editorial said:

Introducing...

NEGRO DIGEST is published in response to a demand for a magazine to summarize and condense the leading articles and comment on the Negro now current in the press of the nation in ever increasing volume.

The impact of the war and attendant discussion of what we are fighting for has focused new attention on the status of the Negro in America. There is wide spread interest in what the Negro thinks of the war, democracy and the South.

In a single, easy-to-read issue, Negro Digest gives you a complete survey of current Negro life and thought. The editors read hundreds of magazines, newspapers, periodicals, books and reports in order to bring you a choice selection of articles and features each month.

Negro Digest is dedicated to the development of interracial understanding and the promotion of national unity. It stands unqualifiedly for the winning of the war and the integration of all citizens into the democratic process.

Negro Digest spoke to an audience that was angry, disillusioned, and disappointed. You couldn't digest that world without digesting the frustration and anger.

13
The Search for a
Common American Market

The first issue of *Negro Digest* was impressive by almost any standard. But I couldn't enjoy it. I'd produced this miracle with smoke and mirrors. And it was time now for a miracle that couldn't be talked or negotiated into existence: money to pay the printer, who discovered on publication day that he'd made a sizable investment in a new and decidedly unpromising company.

I'd ordered five thousand copies, three thousand of which were reserved for prepaid subscribers. I needed to sell the remaining two thousand copies quickly to pay the printing bill and the cost of shipping three thousand copies.

Forty years later, I explained this dilemma to a brilliant student at the Harvard University Business School. He hung on every word and asked breathlessly, obviously expecting a profound answer, "What did you do then?" He was deflated when I told him, "I looked in the Yellow Pages."

The Yellow Pages directed me to the office of Charles Levy Circulating Company, the biggest magazine distributor in Chicago. I was greeted by Joseph Levy, the brother of the original Charles Levy.

I'd rehearsed my appeal, and I rattled it off with perfection, varying the tone, pitch, and emotional level. Joseph Levy listened with a poker face and then said: "Johnson, we don't handle colored books."

Anger wrestled with smartness, and smartness won.

"Is that," I asked innocently, "because you're prejudiced or because colored books don't sell?"

He rose in anger and indignation.

"Johnson, I'm Jewish—I don't believe in prejudice. It's because colored books don't sell."

I told him my magazine was going to sell, and that I would leave my card just in case he changed his mind.

"You can leave it," he said, "but I'm not going to change my mind."

Here, then, was my first major management crisis. How could I change Levy's mind? I could have gone to the NAACP, but that would have taken years of litigation—and I had to sell two thousand magazines quickly or go to jail. I could have gone to Jesse Jackson, but Jesse hadn't been born. So I was on my own. It was up to me to invent an original solution.

This is what I did. I went back to Supreme and asked about thirty of my friends to stop by the Levy outlets on their way home and ask for that exciting new Negro magazine, *Negro Digest*. For almost a week, they visited newsstands, offering money and demanding copies of *Negro Digest*. This was a new and novel civil rights march, and it worked.

Joseph Levy called and said, "I've been getting calls from my dealers. Maybe, Johnson, I'll try a few of those books. About five hundred." I jumped into my car—I was publisher, editor, business manager, circulation manager, and chauffeur—and rushed to his office and persuaded him to take one thousand.

This triumph was tempered by fear. Only a handful of Blacks—my thirty friends—knew the magazines were on the stand. I dipped into my dwindling treasury and gave the thirty friends enough money to buy up all the newsstand copies. This got Levy's attention, and he ordered one thousand additional copies.

Word was circulating on the streets now. If any Black came within a hundred feet of the newsstand, the vendors would call out, "Have you seen the new magazine, *Negro Digest*?" Circulation begat circulation, and I went back to press and printed another five thousand magazines.

Money, which is perhaps the greatest of all civil rights bills, was working now. Levy, who had initially opposed my efforts, now became my biggest booster. He gave me marketing ideas, stressing the importance of distributing flyers at church meetings and social gatherings. He used my placards on his South Side trucks. He said the word that opened the doors of profitable relationships with White distributors in New York, Detroit, and other major cities.

Working together from day to day, Levy and I crossed the artificial barriers that blocked trade and created our own little common market. In the process, we became good friends, and laughed about the problems we had in our first meeting.

What brought us together and made the Levy organization one of the key ingredients in the early success of *Negro Digest* was the realization, never spoken but clearly felt, that racism was a double-edged sword that cut both ways. It cut deeply into my profits and made it impossible for me to cross the economic equator of race. It also cut deeply into his profits and made it impossible for him and other White distributors to maximize their profits in the inner city. For racial divisions kept White distributors from penetrating into the secret nooks and crannies of the close-knit Black community.

To reach these secret places and the mom-and-pop outlets neglected by major distributors, I used Negro-owned distributors in Chicago, Atlanta, Philadelphia, and Los Angeles.

I also developed my own network, relying in most places on postal workers whose unique geo-racial knowledge had never been utilized. They knew the city from throwing mail. Many worked at night and were free in the day.

We recruited agents by running ads in Negro newspapers and by distributing leaflets. Most of the men and women who answered the ads didn't have enough money to buy advance copies. So I created a system that made it possible for agents to order and put the money into the special Negro Digest Publishing Company banking accounts that I opened in several cities.

Local distributors could put money into these accounts but couldn't make withdrawals. I checked these accounts almost daily. At intervals, the money was transferred to my main account in Chicago.

Under this system, which was in place for all of the life of *Negro Digest* and much of the life of *Ebony*, we singlehandedly created a new stratum of Black news dealers and salesmen, much as we would later create new strata of Black photographers, and advertising, marketing, and circulation specialists.

The South was an entirely different problem, for sheriffs and policy chiefs were hostile to all Black media. My approach to this problem was simple and direct. I created a southern network which sold *Negro Digest* and later *Ebony* and *Jet* on buses, streetcars, and even in cottonfields.

Most of these agents used guerrilla tactics, boarding a bus, for example, and working the seats until the next stop. Some, like Thomas Armstrong of Jackson, Mississippi, were beaten and jailed. Nothing, however, stopped them. When we celebrated our fortieth anniversary, we paid a special tribute to the agents of the southern network who did more perhaps than any other American journalists of that era to make the First Amendment real in Dixie.

These and other methods paid off. Within three months, *Negro Digest* was selling in the lucrative New York market. Within six months, the magazine was available on newsstands on the West Coast. Within eight months, we were selling 50,000 copies a month nationally.

Circulation was growing, but I was still running scared. Not knowing from issue to issue how much money I was going to make or lose, I had a sense of budget, a sense of living within my means and of avoiding overhead. For the first year of the operation, I took nothing out and put everything back in.

I am often asked how many issues I published before I made a profit. The answer is simple: if I hadn't made a profit on the first issue, there wouldn't have been a second issue.

The reason I succeeded was that I didn't know that it was impossible to succeed. If I'd known then what MBAs know now, I would have realized that I couldn't start a business that way.

For me, then, ignorance was a blessing. Since I didn't know that it was impossible to do what I wanted to do, I did it.

When *Negro Digest* was published, I didn't have a single full-time employee. I was still employed full-time at Supreme, and I was scared to break that tie because I didn't know how long the *Negro Digest* boom would last. That was part of my insecurity. It was part of my usual practice of running scared.

I finally left Supreme in July 1943, but I didn't make a clean break. I asked for and was given a leave of absence.

Shortly after I left Supreme, I hired my first full-time employee, a secretary. There was no room for her desk in my tiny office, and she had to sit at a desk in the hall. At first, as I later told the War Production Board, "the magazine was a one-man operation. My wife and I did all the work. We gathered the material and edited the magazine. I wrapped the magazines myself, and I hauled them to the post office."

The secretary and I were the only full-time employees until 1944. I disguised this fact by listing free-lancer Ben Burns and my relatives on the masthead. One of the early mastheads listed Burns as associate editor and E. M. Walker and G. J. Williams as assistants. E. M. Walker was my wife's maiden name, and G. J. Williams was my mother.

14
The President's Wife Turns the Tide

Within six months, we were selling more magazines than anyone had thought possible. But we were stuck at a first-stage plateau of 50,000. And magazine circulation, especially in the critical first stage, is like the moon: it either increases or decreases.

What we needed at this crossroads was a major story or gimmick to generate publicity and sales and push us over the next barrier.

I studied the situation and decided that the most promising area of development was one of our regular features, "If I Were a Negro." We were getting a lot of unsolicited advice in this period from Whites, some well-meaning, some not so well-meaning. I decided to take advantage of this trend by asking Whites to put themselves in our shoes and answer some difficult questions.

Would they, for example, want their children to wait another generation for quality education? (That was fifty-three years ago, and the question, God help us, is still relevant.)

Would they want their sons and fathers and brothers to fight Nazi racism in a segregated army?

We posed these and other questions to major figures like Pearl Buck, Orson Welles, and Edward G. Robinson.

Marshall Field, Pearl Buck, and other contributors had attracted some attention, but we needed a bigger attraction. Someone, for example, like Eleanor Roosevelt, who was the wife of the president of the United States and who was denounced somewhere almost every day for talking to Blacks or meeting with Blacks or eating with Blacks.

To get the wife of the president of the United States to write an exclusive article on anything would be a major story for any magazine. But it would be a real coup for a Black magazine to get her to tell what she would do if she were Black.

The idea was pure gold—no doubt about it. But how was I going to get to the wife of the president of the United States? I sat down and thought about it and decided that Mother, as usual, was right. If you want to say something to somebody, write a letter.

I wrote Mrs. Roosevelt and received a prompt reply, saying that she would like to write the article but that she simply didn't have the time. Since she didn't say no, I wrote her again three weeks later. She said she still didn't have the time.

Soon afterward, I read that she was coming to Chicago to speak at what is now the Chicago Hilton. On the day of her scheduled arrival, I sent a telegram—in those days telegrams arrived on time—and asked if she would have a few minutes to dictate the article. I received almost immediately in return a manuscript "written expressly for *Negro Digest*."

People are always telling me that I'm lucky, but luck is a word we use for an order that is not understood. You make some of your luck. You make it by working hard and trusting the logic of events, which always favor the bold and the active and the prepared.

When Eleanor Roosevelt visited our office for the first time, she told us that when my telegram arrived, she had just finished dictating her column, "My Day." She had hardly finished reading the telegram when a sudden change in her schedule made it possible for her to dictate the article. Was that luck or was it the wages of a persistence that refuses to take no for an answer?

The result was an October 1943 cover story by the wife of the president of the United States and marked a major turning point in the fortunes of *Negro Digest*. The president's wife said in the article that if she were a Negro, she would have great bitterness *and* great patience.

Southern White newspapers picked up the part about the great patience. Black newspapers and northern White newspapers picked up the part about great bitterness. And our circulation jumped overnight, from 50,000 to 100,000. After that, we never looked back.

I was making so much money that I didn't know what to do with it. The magazine sold for twenty-five cents on the newsstands. I got about fifteen cents of that, which meant that I made $15,000, give or take a few dollars, from every 100,000 copies sold.

No matter how hard I tried I could only spend $6,000 a month, and the money was piling up. And that, believe it or not, was a problem.

I hired a brilliant young Black CPA, Charles A. Beckett, who introduced me to the mysteries of high finance.

Later, when the company went over the $100-million-a-year mark, I realized for the first time the power and witchery of money. Money can be counted, measured, weighed, but it can't be commanded or predicted.

Always, everywhere, it overflows the experience, giving you more or less than you expected. There's no balance in the life of money. You either have too much or too little. When you don't have it, you run like the devil to get it. And when you have it, you run like the devil to keep it.

Based on Beckett's advice, I plowed most of the money back into the business. In late 1943, I bought my first building, paying $4,000 for it. The building was located at 5619 South State Street.

The first headquarters of Johnson Publishing Company was a typical Chicago storefront with a big plate-glass window facing the sidewalk. My desk was up front inside the plate-glass window, next to the bookkeeping department. That made me happy, for I always wanted to be close to the money.

I bought some used furniture and moved into the new office in November, which was now my lucky month, and started assembling a permanent staff, all of whom worked for me until they died or retired. As the only male executive in a company deemed essential to the war effort, I received a deferment.

I reached out to everybody, for I knew nothing about magazine publishing and editing, how to organize a circulation department or an advertising department, or what forms to use.

I knew nothing about these matters, but by asking and

listening, I found that people, Black and White, will tell you everything you need to know if you confess your ignorance and approach them in the right spirit.

I got a lot of help from friends on the staff of the Catholic magazine *Extension*. I also received advice and assistance from a brilliant young White couple, Jim and M. J. Clement, who read about the new magazine and volunteered their services.

When all else failed, I looked in the phone book and called an expert. Since I had nothing to lose, I always started at the top. I received valuable advice from Henry Luce of *Time-Life* and Gardner Cowles of *Look*.

It was hard to get through to Luce, but I finally convinced his secretary that the only thing I wanted was advice. I've found that you can get through to anybody if you're persistent enough and if you can convince secretaries that you want neither money nor employment.

I used a simple approach that almost always worked. I simply told the secretary or aide that I was the president—I stressed the word *president*—of my company.

"It is," I said, "a small company but I *am* the president, and I want to talk to your president. I'm making this request—from one president to another. If the president of the smallest country in the world comes to Washington, our president, as a matter of public policy and protocol, will see him. So it seems to me that your president, in the American tradition, will see me for a few minutes if you pass this request on and tell him that I don't want a donation or a job."

I used that on Henry Luce's secretary, and I got in to see him. He received me in a big office on one of the upper floors of the old *Time-Life* Building. He was uptight at first, not knowing what to expect and how to react. But he warmed up quickly when I told him what I was trying to do and that I just wanted exposure to *Time-Life* staffers who could tell me whether I was moving in the right direction. He pushed buttons, and editors and business experts came from everywhere. With Luce's blessing, I talked to experts in the New York office and returned to Chicago for discussions with his circulation and promotion departments.

I had a similar experience with Gardner Cowles of *Look*. After I spoke to him in New York, he arranged for me to go to Des Moines, Iowa, to meet with the managers of the magazine's circulation department.

I was secure enough by now to splurge. I made some long-overdue personal investments, buying with a $9,000 down payment my first home, a three-story apartment building.

Eunice and I moved into the first-floor apartment, and my mother and stepfather lived on the second floor. We rented out the third floor.

This was a sound, even conservative, investment. But children, wise men, and fools know that to truly appreciate money it's necessary, from time to time, to spend it on candy or fine wine or love. So I went out and bought three cars—a Buick for my mother, a Buick for my mother-in-law, and a Cadillac for me.

My mother had taken a lot of flak from friends and neighbors. It gave her great joy to go out into the streets and say, "Look! Look what my boy has done for me."

I later did something I'd dreamed of for years: I retired my mother and told her that she'd never have to work again. From that day in 1943 until she died in 1977, a period of thirty-four years, she had a car, chauffeur, and maid, and money and leisure to travel anywhere in the world.

The day I told her that I was putting her on my personal payroll we both broke down in tears. And the feeling of release I had on that day, the feeling of accomplishment—I don't think I've ever had such a feeling, before or since. It was one of those memorable moments when words fail you. I read somewhere that nothing is quite as eloquent as silence. This was a time of silence and tears.

After we moved to the new apartment, I went to a party for Eddie ("Rochester") Anderson, who was in town with Jack Benny. This was one of the rare interracial parties of the time, and I met Robert Wachsman, the publicity agent for Jack Benny and Rochester. Wachsman was an up-front guy with a sense of humor, and we quickly moved from cocktail party chitchat to shared hopes and dreams. I told him that I'd just moved into a new apartment and that I was having a hard time finding an interior decorator.

"You won't believe this," he said, shaking his head, "but my sister-in-law, Viola Marshall Wachsman, is an interior decorator. I'll tell her to call you."

Viola Marshall called, and Eunice and I showed her the apartment and discussed decorating ideas. There was never any doubt after this first discussion that she was the woman for the job. The end result, one of the most tastefully decorated apartments on the North or South Sides, confirmed our judgment.

Viola Marshall was a new phenomenon for us—a well-to-do White woman totally dedicated to racial equality without one iota of racial arrogance. I've only met in my lifetime five or six Whites who were so sure of themselves that they could lift themselves and everybody around them to another realm on the other side of race. Viola Marshall was one of them. I don't think she ever thought about race. And when we were with her, we didn't think about race.

After completing the apartment, she invited us to her Lake Shore Drive apartment for dinner. This was in 1944, and it was almost revolutionary for Blacks to walk into the front door of a Lake Shore Drive apartment as guests. The Black doorman was amazed. The Black maid was flabbergasted. Twenty-three years later, when I saw the scenes of Sidney Poitier and the maid in *Guess Who's Coming to Dinner,* I said out loud, "I've seen this movie before."

When we sat down to dinner in this real-life movie, the maid was very slow in serving the courses. To make sure we got the point, she slammed doors and disappeared into the kitchen for long periods of time. When Viola Marshall asked her what was the problem, she said—and this was undoubtedly the most embarrassing moment of my life—"I don't serve niggers."

"I didn't invite any niggers," Viola Marshall replied. "And if you can't serve my guests, you're fired."

Viola, Eunice, and I served and ate the dinner. She remained a close friend until her death in 1984.

15
The Secret of Success

All through 1943 and 1944, as the Allies pressed German and Japanese forces in Europe and Asia, *Negro Digest* grew, setting new records and new standards for a Black magazine. But progress doesn't run in a straight line. There are zigs and zags and ups and downs. And sometimes it's hard to tell the difference between the two.

When we became too big for the printing press at Progress, I moved to Kallis Printing Company, leaving a $14,000 bill behind. I told the skeptical owner that I was going to pay every penny. He didn't believe me, but I did. This is the foundation of my philosophy: never burn your bridges behind you. Do what's right and leave every job and every situation so you can come back, if you want to.

Is there a reason why we succeeded when so many other Black publishers failed? The answer is yes. I was lucky, we worked hard, and above all, the timing was right.

Victor Hugo said that nothing can stop an idea whose time has come. The time for a Negro magazine, the time for a *Negro Digest* or an *Ebony* or *Jet*, had come and nothing could stop it if someone was willing to do whatever it took to make it succeed.

Can it be done again? Can you start with $500 and build a $200- or $300-million empire?

What is needed is not money but an idea for a business that meets a need that cannot be satisfied elsewhere. If you don't have that, a million dollars won't help you. And if you have it, you have all the money you need.

Scores of Americans, Black and White, have made that discovery. I know a man who made a fortune with a chain of all-night grocery stores. I know a woman who got rich by organizing maids and house cleaners. The chances and the opportunities are as wide as this world.

Another point is relevant here. I didn't start a business to get rich—I started a business to provide a service and to improve myself economically. I think it's a mistake to set out to get rich. You can't get rich trying to get rich. What you need to do is to dream small dreams, because very often when you try to see things in their largest form, you get discouraged, and you feel that it's impossible. But if you can somehow think and dream of success in small steps, every time you make a step, every time you accomplish a small goal, it gives you confidence to go on from there.

I never thought I would be rich. Never in my wildest dreams did I believe that *Negro Digest* would lead to the Johnson Publishing Company of today. If I'd dreamed then of the conglomerate of today, I probably would have been so intimidated, with my meager resources, that I wouldn't have had the courage to take the first step.

All of which brings us back to the question:

Can it be done again?

Yes, it can be done again.

I could do it again.

So could you.

So could any man or woman who comes up with an idea that provides a service no one else is providing and who is willing to subordinate everything to the idea and the dream.

In 1945 I was forced to make a plea that saved the company. I knew I was in trouble when I saw the envelope. It was fat, white, with that black-black type that says Official, Warning, *We got you.*

I ripped open the flap and the first line confirmed my worst fears:

> You are in violation of Regulation L-244. You are hereby ordered to cease and desist publishing the magazine called *Negro Digest* until you reduce your paper usage to your allotted 7.43 tons per quarter.

There was more, a lot more, about certification and notices of appeal. But that was a mere formality. The bottom line was that the U.S. government had John H. Johnson by the throat and had no intention of letting go.

And so it was over, almost before it began.

I had pulled myself up by my bootstraps and had seen, for the first time, some light and green paper at the end of the tunnel. And a bureaucrat who'd never met a payroll in his life was telling me I had to return the boots—and the bootstraps.

That's what the letter meant.

For there was no way I could comply with that order. In April 1945 I was using twenty-five tons of paper a quarter to print 100,000 copies of *Negro Digest*. If I cut back to 7.43 tons per quarter, I would destroy the circulation base of the magazine and wreck my business.

It wasn't fair.

It wasn't equitable.

It wasn't American.

But it was legal.

For a war was going on, and the government controlled almost everything, including paper, which was parceled out according to a nothing-keeps-nothing formula. If, for example, you were using twenty-five tons of paper in October 1942—a month before *Negro Digest* was founded—you could use twenty-five tons of paper in 1945. If, on the other hand, you were using zero tons of paper in 1942, you could use zero tons of paper in 1945.

All this was as clear as the Washington Monument. It had been written down and published in the trade papers. And ignorance of the law was no defense. There was even a Catch-22 provision. To get paper to print your magazine, you had to sign a paper saying that you'd read and understood Order L-244.

The bureaucrat who signed the letter came down hard on the Catch-22 provision. He wanted to know how I obtained additional tons of paper. He used the ugly word "collusion" and hinted at penalties or worse for willful violation of the code and—this was the stinger—impeding the war effort.

I had a sudden vision of prison bars. And I ran to the

nearest lawyer, who told me that it was too heavy for him and that I needed a specialist who knew the ins and outs of the War Production Board. I talked to my printer who said he was a member of the Graphic Arts Association, which retained a lawyer named J. Norman Goddess.

"Talk to him," the printer said. "He's supposed to help our customers."

I took the letter to Goddess and told him I wanted to hire him to go with me to the appeals hearing in Washington. Goddess, a tall, stooped White man who never rushed or hurried, read the letter and looked at me the way a doctor looks at a patient with a new and interesting—and terminal—disease. He read the letter again and looked at me again, this time with the consoling look that surgeons, ministers, and undertakers give the next of kin.

Since he wouldn't say it, I said it.

"I'm in trouble, and I need the best lawyer I can find."

He corrected me.

"You're in so much trouble that the best lawyer in the world can't help you. You've been violating an admittedly unjust law. You've signed two documents which say that you knew that you were violating the law. If you go to Washington with a lawyer, you compound what has been done, and the board will eat you and the lawyer alive."

"What can I do, then?"

"There's only one thing you can do but uh—uh—uh...." He turned red and started shuffling papers on his desk.

I knew what the problem was. The problem was the live wire of race which intrudes on the most private relations of Blacks and Whites, short-circuiting communications between husbands and wives, doctors and patients, lawyers and clients. Goddess had something to say to me, man-to-man, and nothing in his past, none of his law books or cases, had prepared him for the task of eliminating the White man / Black man barrier. I waited, knowing that there was no future in our relationship if he couldn't cross this new and dangerous road by himself.

"I hope you're not offended," he said finally, dropping his

voice. "I won't go to the Washington hearing with you, and the best legal advice I can give you is that you should pretend that you've had no legal advice." He added:

"The law set up a paper quota based on what was used in the first months after you started your magazine. Since you could only use 7.43 tons in the first months, you're stuck with 7.43 tons. But the law says that in cases of extreme hardship, the board may, at its own discretion, grant relief and permit you to continue publishing."

He pulled his chair closer to me and crossed the great divide, saying:

"If I were you, I would go down to Washington alone, and I would be—please don't be offended—a poor colored man who knows nothing about these complicated laws. Your only hope now is to create confusion and sympathy for you and your plight."

I took this advice and walked into Room 5066 of the Railroad Retirement Building in Washington, D.C., on Tuesday, June 12, 1945, without a lawyer or a legal pad. Twenty-five people appeared before the Appeals Board of the War Production Board on that day. Most came with lawyers, CPAs, marketing experts, charts and graphs.

I came with fear and trembling and a cry for help. The other petitioners were fighting for an economic advantage; I was fighting for my life. If their appeal was rejected, they would go on to something else. If my appeal was rejected, I was going back to the edge. So I sat there aware of the bump, bump, bump of my heart, and waited for the War Production Appeals Board to hear Docket No. R-375:

APPEAL BY
THE NEGRO DIGEST
CHICAGO, ILLINOIS

FROM ORDER L-244 of the
PRINTING AND PUBLISHING
DIVISION

I had rehearsed my appeal a thousand times, but when Docket No. R-375 was called, my plea was spontaneous— from the heart. I told the five members of the board how hard I'd worked to start my magazine, how much it meant to me personally, and to Black people in general. I told them I needed a production of 100,000 copies to keep my organization intact and to permit me to discharge my debts until the inevitable victory of our brave solders permitted the lifting of paper restrictions.

"We feel," I said, "that to limit us to the quota which has been recommended would not only work a hardship on the magazine as a corporation, but it would also work a hardship on our distributors, many of whom gave up other positions in order to get into this type of work."

Magazine content was not considered a basis for appeal. It was unrealistic, I said, to ignore the racial tensions in America and what *Negro Digest* was doing to try to ease them.

"We have attracted a number of persons—Negroes and Whites—who have contributed articles which we believe have improved racial relations. We have printed articles about the history and achievement of the Negro, and these have bolstered the morale of the men in service...."

As I talked, I noticed, out of the corner of my eye, that one member of the board—C. Osborn, whom I later learned was an entrepreneur and publisher himself—was nodding his head and smiling. Recalling my debating class at DuSable High School, I talked directly to him.

"I believe," I said, "that putting us out of business, which this quota would effectively do, would create an unusual hardship not only for us, but it would set the Negro magazine publishing field back a good many years. I wouldn't be able to go around and explain to each member of the group who has been funding the magazine that we were denied an appeal by the War Production Board. They would assume that for some financial reason we were discontinuing publication, which would make it unusually difficult for a new magazine to begin after the war because these people would say, 'I invested my money in the *Negro Digest* and it failed....' "

So far, so good. But what about the clear language of Order L-244? What about the regulations established by the War Production Board to further the war effort?

I told the board that I was not a member of "any publishers' association, and...did not have direct access to information regarding these orders."

Why wasn't I a member of the all-White publishers' association? Why didn't I have direct access to the conventions and luncheons and country clubs of the publishers? I didn't raise these questions. By not raising them, I said to the members of the Appeals Board that *we* know why I didn't have *direct* (code word) access to the information.

A lawyer who read the transcript told me that Thurgood Marshall on his best day as an advocate couldn't have done any better. More to the point, my advocate on the board, C. Osborn, expressed his approval. When the chairman asked for questions from members of the board, Osborn said: "I would like to first compliment the appellant on his excellent presentation, and to say that my sympathies would certainly be in the direction of a one-man magazine publisher because I was one myself once." He then had me read into the record Section F-8 which authorized exceptions for "unforeseen, unusual, extraordinary or emergency conditions constituting undue and excessive hardship."

The Consultant of the Magazine Section of the Printing and Publishing Division of the War Production Board recommended denial of the appeal. But Osborn and the board overruled him and granted my twenty-five tons a quarter.

Of the twenty-five persons who appeared before the board on that Tuesday in 1945, only John Johnson, who came without counsel and who had to win or go out of business, prevailed. And it seemed to me as I walked out of that building into the suddenly bright Washington light that there was a sign or a portent in this, and that somebody or something was trying to tell me that God and history had blessed this venture. At any rate, I went back to Chicago and hired J. Norman Goddess. A lawyer who knows that no lawyer is sometimes the best lawyer is a lawyer you ought to have on your payroll.

Now that the future of *Negro Digest* was assured, I turned my attention to the proposal for the magazine that became *Ebony*. I wish I could say that it was my idea. But I had my hands full with *Negro Digest* and was in no mood to embark on a new venture.

The first suggestion for another magazine came from my two principal freelancers, Jay Jackson and Ben Burns, who had been pestering me for weeks with an idea for a new entertainment-oriented magazine. They wanted to call the magazine *Jive*.

I had no interest in *Jive*, but to keep two valued contributors happy I said I would go into a three-way partnership. We decided to put up $1,000 each and split the profits three ways. But at put-up time, neither Jackson nor Burns had the money.

"Well," I said, "we've gone this far and we might as well see the hole card. But if I have to put in all the money, then I have to own the whole thing."

Both men agreed. They said they would go along with the deal if I would pay them more money for their freelance work.

We shook hands, and the rest, as they say, is history.

Ben Burns and Jay Jackson got a raise in pay, and John Johnson got a new magazine.

But it wasn't going to be the magazine that Burns and Jackson had proposed.

"Now that the magazine is mine," I said, "I'm going to put out something entirely different. I don't like the name 'Jive' and I don't like the 'Jive' audience. I've been thinking a lot about picture magazines. I've been doing some crude market research, checking newsstands in the Black community, and dealers tell me that the only magazine selling almost as much as *Negro Digest* in Black communities is *Life*. I think the time is ripe for a Black picture magazine."

There was another argument in favor of a Black picture magazine:

"The war will soon be over and Black vets will be coming home, looking for more glamour and more pizzazz than we're running in *Negro Digest*. They'll need a period of relaxation and relief from the day-to-day combat with racism."

This was a crucial turning of the road in my personal and corporate life, and I almost missed it. For if Ben Burns and Jay Jackson had come up with their thousand-dollar shares, *Ebony* probably would not have been published.

So I got the keys to a gold mine by default. Once I got into the thing and realized the hidden potential, I began to get more excited. The more excited I became, the more I realized that fate, which knows us better than we know ourselves, had dragged me, protesting and screaming, onto the freeway of the future.

There's something in human nature that fastens like a leech on what worked yesterday. And the executive suites of America are filled with men and women who have been disqualified for tomorrow's success by yesterday's success. Most of the problems of American industry, including the failure to anticipate and adapt to changes in the electronic and car industries, can be traced to the fatal disease "WWY"—what worked yesterday.

The road from *Negro Digest* to *Jive* to *Ebony* cured me of that disease and taught me that you are only as good as your next success. It taught me that no matter how well you're doing and no matter how well you've done, you've got to keep your eyes open for new opportunities.

Show me a man or woman who's satisfied with what he or she's got, and I'll show you a man or woman who's not going to get anything else and is in danger of losing what he or she has. I speak from personal experience here. For if I had continued to rely on *Negro Digest* alone, I would be out of business today.

Change. That's the only thing that never changes.

That's what Longfellow meant when he said there are no birds in yesterday's nest.

It's what Duke Ellington meant when he said that "things ain't what they used to be."

A good businessman knows that. He anticipates change, prepares for change, and rides the winds of change. He puts himself in the consumer's place and walks a mile or farther in his or her shoes. From that vantage point, he tries to see what the consumer sees and to want what he wants.

And let there be no misunderstanding here: it's not enough to sit in a big office and read reports and study bar graphs. You've got to get out of your office and walk the streets with customers and sell products with your salesmen. Somebody said once that "in order to get lion's cubs, you have to go into the lion's lair." I'm no expert on lions, but I know people, and I tell you there's no other way to keep up with their changing needs.

I met a woman in a community supermarket who was shocked to find me pushing a cart down the aisles and taking canned goods off the shelves.

"You shouldn't be doing this," she said. "You should have an aide shop for you."

I told her, "I do this because I like to do it." I could have added that I do it because it's a good way to keep your finger on the pulse of consumers.

People are always asking me what kind of business I'm going into next. I always say I don't know. How could I know until people tell me what product they're going to demand next? To find out what they're going to demand next, I keep a finger in the air, an ear to the ground, and both eyes on the marching throng. What I'm looking for is a target of opportunity. When it presents itself, I act.

That's the only way to run a business in the modern world. You can't be satisfied with yesterday's success, no matter how enjoyable or satisfying it might be. And you're a fool if you think that what you did yesterday is going to satisfy your customers or your board or your wife forever.

There was another marker on the road to *Ebony*, and that was a change in the world's color guard. By 1945 we had come to a great divide in world history, and this was reflected in the changing geography of media. The great Negro weekly newspapers—and the great White dailies—had by this time reached their peak and were giving way to the blitzkrieg of the photograph, first in *Life* and *Look*, and then in television.

I survived TV and the age of the photograph, and invested in a new journalism that made it possible for Black media to weather the storms of change. My moves were dictated not by abstract theories but by hunches that came from the deepest layers of my psyche. I can see with the benefit of 20/20 hindsight that the Black newspaper publishers were making the same mistake in neglecting pictures that I was making in holding on to the successful *Negro Digest* idea.

People wanted to see themselves in photographs. White people wanted to see themselves in photographs, and Black people wanted to see themselves in photographs. We were dressing up for society balls, and we wanted to see that. We were going places we had never been before and doing things we'd never done before, and we wanted to see that.

We wanted to *see* Dr. Charles Drew and Ralph Bunche and Jackie Robinson and the other men and women who were on the cutting edge of tomorrow. We wanted to know where they lived, what their families looked like, and what they did when they weren't on stage.

The picture magazines of the forties did for the public what television did for the audiences of the fifties: they opened new windows in the mind and brought us face to face with the multicolored possibilities of man and woman. The more I dealt with photographs, the more I understood their importance. I didn't see it in the beginning, but, step by step, I began to understand the revolutionary importance of the new journalism.

Out of these bits and pieces evolved the *Ebony* philosophy. We wanted to emphasize the positive aspects of Black life. We wanted to highlight achievements and make Blacks proud of themselves. We wanted to create a windbreak that would let them get away from "the problem" for a few moments and say, "here are some Blacks who are making it. And if they can make it, I can make it, too."

We started out saying, in effect, that Black newspapers were doing a good job of reporting discrimination and segregation and that we needed, in addition to that, a medium to refuel the people, and to recharge their batteries. We needed, in addition to traditional weapons, a medium to make Blacks believe in themselves, in their skin color, in their noses, in their lips, so they could hang on and fight for another day. Last but not least, we needed a new medium—bright, sparkling, readable—that would let Black Americans know that they were part of a great heritage.

This was the idea.

We intended to highlight Black breakthroughs and pockets of progress. But we didn't intend to ignore difficulties and harsh realities. We intended to call a spade a spade and an ace an ace. And we intended to say, always and everywhere, that they are part of the same deck and can't be understood in isolation from each other.

Beyond all that, we wanted to focus on the total Black experience—something no one else was doing then and, I am tempted to say, now. For Black people, in addition to being members of the NAACP and National Urban League, were also members of sororities and fraternities and lodges. They marched and partied but they also raised children and gave debutante balls and watched baseball and football games.

We wanted to show Negroes—we were Negroes then— and Whites the Negroes nobody knew.

If you had relied on the White press of that day, you would have assumed that Blacks were not born, because the White press didn't deal with our births.

You would have assumed that we didn't finish school, because the White press didn't deal with our educational achievements.

You would have assumed that we didn't get married, because the White press didn't print our wedding announcements or pictures of Black brides and grooms cutting cakes.

You would have assumed that we didn't die, because it didn't deal with our funerals.

Back then, at the ending of World War II, the idea and the dream were on the defensive in the media and the streets. There were no Black mayors in major cities then, and there were no Blacks in organized baseball. Or organized football. Or organized basketball.

You won't believe this, but people said then, in all serious-
ness, that Blacks were biologically incapable of playing on the
Brooklyn Dodgers and the Chicago Bears and the New York
Knicks.

This was the situation in 1945.

This was the year the United Nations was founded with
Black American participation.

This was the year the lights went on again in the hearts of
Black and Brown people all over the world.

This was the year America and the world changed forever.

Jesse Jackson was four years old.

Sidney Poitier was eighteen.

Martin Luther King, Jr. was sixteen.

And I was twenty-seven.

Nat King Cole was singing "Straighten Up and Fly Right."
And Charlie Parker, the apostle of the new sound, was playing
"Now Is the Time."

They were jitterbugging in that year at the Apollo and the
Regal and the Howard, but they were also dreaming and marching and mobilizing.

This was the world that *Ebony* was born to portray. And I
recall it not to cast stones but to emphasize how far the idea
and the dream have traveled. For *Ebony* was founded in that
far-away world to testify to the possibilities of a new and
different world.

In a world of despair, we wanted to give hope.

In a world of negative Black images, we wanted to provide
positive Black images.

In a world that said Blacks could do few things, we wanted
to say they could do everything.

We believed in 1945 that Black Americans needed positive
images to fulfill their potential. We believed then—and we
believe now—that you have to change images before you can
change acts and institutions.

This, in brief, was the prospectus for the new magazine:
words and pictures, *Black* words and pictures, and a complete

presentation of the Black image, showing professionals and entertainers, athletes and doctors and preachers and women and men and children, everybody. This was the idea.

The only problem was the name. If not "Jive," then what? Since we could not register a name that was fully descriptive of the product, we started looking for a word that meant *black* but didn't mean magazine. I discussed the problem with Eunice, who has an arts background and keeps up with new developments in the field. By coincidence, she'd been reading some material on design and color.

"What about 'ebony'?" she asked. "It means fine black African wood."

End of search.

And the beginning of a real-life adventure that has given new meaning and new color to an old name.

The name means, as Eunice said, a tree, the hard, heavy, fine black wood that the tree yields, and the ambiance and mystique surrounding the tree and the color.

The magazine would become so successful that the word would also mean the magazine published by and for Black Americans.

We had a name and an idea. The only thing lacking was paper, which wouldn't be available, the War Production Board said, until the Japanese were defeated.

While we were waiting, we made mock-ups and went through dry runs and watched the world turn.

On April 12, Franklin Delano Roosevelt died.

On May 7, Germany surrendered.

On August 15, Japan surrendered.

On November 1, I published Vol. 1, No. 1 of *Ebony* magazine. The 13¼ by 9¾ inch magazine sold for twenty-five cents. The first cover was a black-and-white photograph of seven boys (six Whites and one Black) from New York's Henry Street Settlement. The cover story, "Children's Crusade," was a first-person piece by the Reverend A. Ritchie Low, a White pastor who was trying to eliminate bias by taking Harlem Blacks to Vermont farms for their annual vacation. Reading this story today, you realize suddenly that the world of 1945 was an innocent world, bright with a hope that is no longer available to people who have lived through Birmingham and Watts and Memphis.

There were fifteen stories in the fifty-two-page magazine. There was a profile on novelist Richard Wright and a story on a Black businessman who went from "slave to banker." We also highlighted "Catholics and Color," "The Truth About Brazil," and "Jam Session in Movieland."

People said then and they say now that we only dealt with the "happy" side. But we talked turkey, then and now. The first *Ebony* photo-editorial called for "Sixty million jobs or else...." It's ironic that Black unemployment is even more of a problem forty-four years later.

The first issue had the same flair and format as the White picture magazines. But there was one major difference. There was not a single ad in the whole issue.

I took the high road from the beginning, announcing that I wouldn't accept ads until we had a guaranteed circulation of 100,000. I had never asked for anything I was not entitled to. I had never asked for charity or handouts, and I had no intention of starting in 1945. I also discouraged the small and unsightly "charm" and "reader"-type ads that had been the staple of the Negro press.

No one believed me. They laughed at my plans and pretensions. But nobody could mistake my message. I intended to go first class. I wanted the big four-color ads that were the staple of the White magazines.

The public response to the new magazine was immediate and spectacular. The first press run of 25,000 was sold out in hours, and we went back to press and printed another 25,000.

Based on cash orders, the magazine said in its December issue, *Ebony* had taken "the circulation championship among Negro magazines away from the longtime title-holder, its sister *Negro Digest*," and was now "the biggest Negro magazine in the world in both size and circulation." *Ebony* has held that title now for forty-four years. The press run has grown from the original 25,000 to more than 2 million. The magazine has grown from a readership of some 125,000 an issue to more than 9 million per issue, and it is the flagship of a miniconglomerate that grosses more than $200 million a year.

The reason for the magazine's success was plain. We were giving people something they wanted and couldn't get anywhere else—a basic formula for success in any business. From Jackson, Mississippi, from Oakland, California, from Harlem and Washington and Atlanta, from cities and hamlets all over America, came the same message: "We've never seen ourselves before in large photographs presented in a positive light unrelated to crime, and we love it."

Our first four-color cover (March 1946) featured a luscious Lena Horne and sold 275,000 copies. The issue was hardly on the streets when an excited woman called and asked to speak to the editor. The editor wasn't in, and she told the switchboard operator, "That picture of Lena Horne in color...is just like a drink of champagne."

A handful of people objected to the name *Ebony* and were answered in the fourth issue, which posed the question: "What's in a name?"

We said:

> Whether ebony is an African wood, a concerto [Stravinsky's "Ebony Concerto"], a nightclub or a magazine, we think it's a good name—alive, dramatic, exciting, colorful.
>
> There's nothing wrong with black....As a race, Negroes have much to be proud of. Their achievements stamp black as a color to take pride in. Black is and should be a color of high esteem....We hope to teach through the medium of *Ebony* what the word means.

The White press had ignored the birth of *Negro Digest,* but *Ebony* was a mountain that commanded attention. *Time* welcomed the new magazine with a story entitled "The Brighter Side."

The *Newsweek* story ("Ebony With Pictures") said the new magazine, "which follows the format of *Life* and *Look*," was a "slick-paper job...crammed with pictures of such Negro celebrities as Rochester (Eddie Anderson), the radio comedian; Hazel

Scott, the pianist; Richard Wright, the novelist; and Maj. R. R. Wright, the banker."

An embarrassingly small number of people produced the first issue. There were only three names on the masthead: editor and publisher John H. Johnson, executive editor Ben Burns, and art editor Jay Jackson.

Within two months, I hired three additional persons. My accountant, Charles A. Beckett, came on temporarily as business manager to organize the business department. Allan Morrison and Kay Cremin were hired as associate editors.

Later that year, I hired Robert Lucas, who'd written for radio shows and confession magazines, and Freda DeKnight, a New York City caterer who inaugurated our "Date With a Dish" feature. In addition, we used big-name writers like Langston Hughes and world-class photographers like Stephen Deutch, Wayne Miller, and Phil Stern. One of the highlights of our first issue was a spectacular photographic essay on jazz by Gjon Mili.

There was not enough room in the State Street Office for our growing staff, and so we leased an additional two-story building. It was on South Calumet. We transferred the editorial, circulation, and business departments to the Calumet Street office and used the State Street facility for warehousing and shipping.

The new central office was relatively small, ten thousand feet or so. The staff was small and close-knit. We were all young, we had the same hopes and aspirations, and we were on the greatest of all highs—the high of making a new thing, of blazing a new path, of going where no Black or White had been.

There was no sharp line between departments or managers and staff people. At lunchtime, the whole staff would troop to Walgreens drugstore, put a couple of tables together, and continue animated discussions about the contents of the next issue.

We weren't editing a magazine; we were on a crusade. And our excitement was contagious. It permeated our lives and spilled over into the pages of the magazine, which attracted large numbers of readers who acted like converts or fans. It was a heady and exciting time, and almost every issue became a milestone.

In May 1946, we accepted our first ads.

In August 1946, we published our first food feature, "Barbecue Chicken." The "Date With a Dish" title was used for the first time in October 1946 ("How to Glorify the Apple").

In October 1946, we started using the facilities of Hall Printing Company, one of the world's largest printers.

In July 1947, we became the first Black magazine audited by the Audit Bureau of Circulation, which reported peak net paid sales of 309,715 in the final quarter of 1946. This was the largest circulation of any Black publication in the world.

There were only two small problems on the editorial side. A story on Joe Louis made the champ fighting mad. He sued, saying we'd attacked his manhood and his honor.

I was embarrassed, not only because of the threat to the new venture but also because I truly admired Joe. Although he'd been denied a formal education by the Old South, he was one of the most educated and thoughtful men I've ever met. He was capable of great eloquence. What athlete—or politician, for that matter—has given a better definition of the limits of evasion and retreat: "He can run but he can't hide." When, during World War II, preachers and leaders said we were going to win because God was on our side, Joe corrected them, saying: "We're going to win because we're on God's side."

A public fight was not in Joe's interest or my interest, and I called him and told him so.

"Johnny," Joe said, "I don't want to hurt you—I just don't want you attacking me. Whenever anybody attacks me, I fight back."

What did Joe want?

"If you'll apologize," he said, "and pay my attorney's fees, I'll drop the suit."

I apologized. If I've learned anything in the last fifty years, I've learned that the best way to deal with a mistake is to admit you made a mistake. Don't waffle. Don't make excuses. Don't explain. Open your mouth, say you're sorry.

People appreciate that approach. They appreciate executives and politicians who are big enough to fold a bad hand and walk away, without making excuses and without looking back.

My mother, who didn't play cards but who knew when to hold and fold the cards of life, taught me an even more important lesson.

"If you make a mistake," she said, "and you're going to make mistakes, because you're not God, the best thing to do is to admit it publicly, put it behind you, and get on with the business of life."

It's human to make mistakes, and readers and customers know it. What they dislike is dishonesty and attempts to defend the indefensible.

I didn't try to defend the editor who wrote the Joe Louis story. I apologized privately and publicly, and Joe and I became friends again and remained friends until his death. When he died in 1981, *Ebony* published a five-page salute to The Champ.

The only other problem we faced on the editorial side was a national coal strike which shut down some departments at the printing press and made us miss the June 1946 issue of *Ebony*. With that one exception, I have never in forty-seven years of publishing missed an issue, or a payroll.

Despite the coal strike and the temporary setback of the Joe Louis suit, the *Ebony* plow continued to open new furrows, printing stories that can be consulted today with profit, such as our pioneering career series: "Negro Lawyers," 1,300 in April 1947 compared with 24,000 in 1988; "Negro Profs at White Colleges," "60-odd" in October 1947 compared with 10,000 in 1988; "Lady Lawyers," 70 in August 1947 compared with 10,000 in 1988; "Negroes on White Dailies," "15-odd" in April 1948 and 2,136 in 1988.

It's difficult to believe that there were only sixteen Black disc jockeys in December 1947, and some future historian will probably find it difficult to believe that there are an estimated five thousand today. We thought we were saying something in May 1948 when we identified "an army" of forty "Brown Hucksters" selling goods and services for American corporations. But it's impossible to count the Black salesmen and sales representatives today.

We were among the earliest and most passionate defenders of Black beauty. We were fascinated by the different hues (smoke, cinnamon, chocolate, cream, golden, pecan, coffee) in the Black rainbow, and we were astonished by the inability of White Americans to appreciate that beauty. We didn't apologize for it—it was a part of our mission, as we noted in our May 1946 issue.

"Beauty," we said, "is skin-deep—and that goes for brown as well as white skin. You'd never think it, though, to look at the billboards, magazine, and pinup posters of America."

We asked George Karger, one of the top photographers of the forties, to capture the beauty of a Black woman. And to make the comparison even more complete, we selected a beautiful and scholastically brilliant young woman, Barbara Gonzales, the first Black to graduate from Sarah Lawrence College.

Even in this early period, *Ebony* was getting great reviews from its contemporaries such as *Reader's Digest*, *Saturday Review of Literature*, and *Tide*, the advertising and marketing magazine. One of the *Reader's Digest* top editors came to Chicago to negotiate the price for a reprint from *Ebony*.

"What about $500?" he asked.

I was shocked into silence; I had no idea that magazines paid that much for articles. The editor misinterpreted my silence and said, "What about $1,000? Would that be all right?" I said yes, and he reached into his pocket and pulled out two checks, one for $500 and the other for $1,000. He gave me the $1,000 check and returned the $500 check to his pocket with a smile.

I learned something that day. Never accept a first offer, and don't make your move too soon.

It was clear by our sixth issue that we were more than a magazine. To our readers, some of whom apparently believed we were capable of miracles, we were a combination general store, service bureau, and post exchange.

Family came first

Gertrude Johnson Williams, Johnson's mother, as a young woman.

John Johnson as a young commencement speaker, Du Sable High School, 1936.

Wedding party, Selma, Alabama, June 21, 1941. (Art Craft Studio)

First child, John H. Johnson Jr., 1957. (Leroy Jeffries)

Daughter Linda's wedding, 1984. (Dave Schuessler)

With Henry Luce, founder and publisher of *Time* and *Life* magazines.

Admiring 20th anniversary cake with Thurgood Marshall, Lena Horne, and Arthur Godfrey, 1965. (Moneta Sleet, Jr.)

Chairman and CEO with Eunice, the secretary-treasurer, and Linda, the president and chief operating officer. (James L. Mitchell)

First office of Johnson Publishing in small law library on 2nd floor, 1942.

From a tiny office to a giant corporation

Company's second office, 1943.

First major office building and the home office staff, 1955.

Johnson Publishing Company Building, 1972.
First office building constructed in downtown
Chicago by a Black-owned corporation.
(Norman L. Hunter)

With President John F. Kennedy and Jacqueline Kennedy, attending celebration of the Emancipation Proclamation, 1963.

John Johnson meets the Presidents

With President Lyndon Johnson, 1964. (Maurice Sorrell)

With President Richard Nixon, 1969. (Official White House Photograph)

With President Gerald Ford, 1971.
(Maurice Sorrell)

With President Jimmy Carter, 1983

With President Ronald Reagan, and USSR General Secretary Michail Gorbachev, 1987
(Official White House Photograph)

With President George Bush. (Official White House Photograph)

With Bill Clinton while he was Governor of Arkansas, 1986. (James L. Mitchell)

Meeting with world leaders

With Golda Meir in Nairobi, Kenya, 1963. (Moneta Sleet, Jr.)

With President Jomo Kenyatta at Kenya Independence Celebration, 1963. (Moneta Sleet, Jr.)

At Ghana Independence Celebration with Prime Minister Kwame Nkrumah, 1957. (Moneta Sleet, Jr.)

With civil rights leader Jesse L. Jackson, 1987. (Vandell Cobb)

Eunice and John with British Prime Minister Margaret Thatcher, 1988. (Official White House Photograph)

Supporting a good cause with Oprah Winfrey and Coretta Scott King, 1989.

Meeting with celebrities

With Elizabeth Taylor and Senator John Warner, 1981.

Sharing a joke with Bill Cosby, 1983.

With Mayor Harold Washington at celebration of Chicago's 150th anniversary. (D. Michael Cheer)

Celebrating the fiftieth anniversary of the National Urban League with Governor Nelson A. Rockefeller (right), New York Mayor Robert F. Wagner (second from left), and League Executive Director Lester B. Granger, 1960.

Special Ambassador Johnson with Robert Kennedy and other members of the U.S. delegation at Ivory Coast Independence Celebration, 1961. (G. Marshall Wilson)

Recieving NAACP's coveted Spingarn Award, 1966.

17
"Failure Is a Word I Don't Accept"

We were a legend after only six months of publication.

And it seemed on the surface that everything was going my way.

I was turning deals left and right. I had two hot magazines, and I was selling 400,000 copies a month.

I had it made.

Right?

Wrong.

Success was killing me.

The more *Ebonys* I sold, the more money I lost. And bills were piling up. I owed the printer and the engraver and suppliers all over town.

They were singing my praises in Harlem and Hollywood, and I was hiding in my office to avoid my creditors.

The problem was obvious to anyone who could read a balance sheet. I was selling too many magazines without a supporting advertising foundation, and I was confronted with three interlocking problems.

The first was the economics of slick paper. Which cost money. Big money.

The second problem was the economics of printing a magazine with quality reproduction on million-dollar presses. Again money. Big money.

The third problem was the economics of numbers. 200,000 magazines with slick paper and good reproduction require more trees, ink, and postage stamps than 100,000 magazines. 300,000 magazines cost more than 200,000.

And so on.

The situation would have been funny if it hadn't been so serious. The glamorous *Ebony* was getting all the attention, and all the praise, but the steady, undramatic *Negro Digest*, 100,000 to 150,000 copies monthly with relatively small production costs, was paying the bills. But there was a limit to the debt structure *Negro Digest* could carry. The runaway success of *Ebony* was stretching the *Negro Digest* corset to its breaking point. And if *Negro Digest* collapsed, John H. Johnson and the whole structure were going down with it.

Why didn't I rein in *Ebony* and cut back on its growth?

I couldn't. It was a simple matter of arithmetic. The more *Ebony* readers, the more potential advertisers.

Why didn't I walk away from the *Ebony* sweepstakes? You've got to be kidding. Walk away from a potential gold mine that dwarfed anything I'd ever dreamed of?

No way.

There was no way I was going to give up a publication which had grown in a short time from 25,000 to nearly half a million. I wasn't confused. I knew what I was doing. The only question was: could I find continuous advertising support before the new magazine wrecked me and my company?

And so, as we headed into the backstretch of 1946—the most dangerous and difficult year in my personal and corporate life—my position was roughly this: I had a tiger by the tail and I couldn't afford to hang on or let it go.

For the moment—for a *brief* moment—I considered the possibility of failure. But the mere thought of the word made my body shake and my heart pound, and I banished it once and for all from my life and vocabulary.

I remember firing a young man for using the word *failure*.

"Nothing personal," I said, "but I'm too insecure myself to have people around me who believe that failure is a possibility. Failure is a word that I don't accept."

I dismissed another associate who kept trying to tell me that I couldn't make it.

"I've got to fire you," I said. "I'm not sure I can make it myself. The last thing I need is someone telling me that I can't make it."

Failure: I was at war with the word and all its variations.

The word I wanted to hear, then and now, was *success*. The energy I sought, then and now, was the energy that comes from focusing all your powers, like a beam, on a single point.

I used to lock myself up in my office and say the word *success* out loud, over and over, like a Buddhist monk chanting his mantra. I used to say to myself, "John Johnson, you can make it. John Johnson, you can make it. John Johnson, you can make it, John Johnson, *you can and must make it.*"

When things got very tough, I'd call my mother and she would say, "You can make it."

I told her one day in perhaps the worst week of my life, "Mother, it looks like I'm going to fail."

"Son," she said, "are you trying hard?"

"Yes."

"*Real* hard?"

"Yes."

"Well," she said, closing the conversation, "whenever you're trying hard, you're never failing. The only failure is failing to try."

I also called Mary McLeod Bethune, the former National Young Administration (NYA) executive who headed Bethune-Cookman College. Mrs. Bethune, who was another one of the most unforgettable characters I've known, was short and black as polished ebony. She was not what the world considers beautiful, but she had so much soul force and authority that when she walked into a room all eyes were pulled to her, as if to a magnet. I was a graduate of her NYA program, and she considered me one of her boys. It was only natural for me to turn to her when the difficulties mounted.

"Hang on," she told me. "Have faith, keep trying." She paused and added:

"The project is too good to end, the Lord wouldn't want it to end."

Years later, when I met W. Clement Stone for the first time, I told him, "I've been practicing PMA—Positive Mental Attitude—since I started my first business. I didn't know what to call it, and I didn't know how to define it, but I was doing it—and it helped me survive."

The reason I survived is that I refused to believe the signs that said I was defeated. And I dared to do things I couldn't afford to do.

And I'm convinced that the only way to get ahead in this world is to live and sell dangerously. You've got to live beyond your means. You've got to commit yourself to an act or a vision that pulls you further than you want to go and forces you to use your hidden strengths.

For you're stronger than you think you are. And what you need—what all men and women need—is an irrevocable act that forces you, on pain of disgrace, jail, or death, to be the best you that you can be.

I was driven by the fear of going back. And I was forced, in the absence of conventional financing, to develop creative financing techniques. One technique was to put off paying bills until the last possible moment. I developed a sixth sense about the limits of delay. I told my staff that I always paid my bill just before my credit went bad.

Why didn't I go to the bank and get a loan?

Because banks didn't lend money to Blacks in those days. I was in business twenty years before I got a loan from a bank. And I was in business forty years before I got what I consider a White man's loan—a loan based on my signature alone.

For two years, from November 1945 to November 1947, I walked a tightrope without a net, pyramiding creditors, postponing bills, stalling, improvising, selling. Perhaps the strangest aspect of this strange season is that some of my warmest relationships were with the people I owed the most money. There was the paper mill executive who extended credit far beyond the known or potential resources of my company.

The bill became so large that the executive developed anxiety attacks that could only be stilled by listening to me explain how I was going to pay the bill. He called me in one day and said, "Your bill is getting bigger and bigger and I want to know what your plans are. I mean, how soon will you be able to sell some advertising and get things under control and reduce your obligations to us?"

Sincerity is perhaps the greatest selling force in the world. And I was sincere in wanting to survive and get a handle on

Ebony, which was like a runaway horse, hurtling down the streets and pulling me behind it.

I explained all this to the executive. He was all right as long as I was talking to him but I had to call him every day and tell him how many ads I'd sold, how great the future looked, and how I planned to pay the bill. It was almost like a fix that I had to give him every day so he could survive.

I made the mistake one day of going to New York without calling him and the roof fell in. My secretary finally reached me in New York, and there was this breathless voice on the phone, saying, "Johnson, tell me again, how do you plan to pay this bill?"

I developed many techniques for keeping him satisfied. If I had a $5,000 payment to make, I wouldn't pay it all at one time—I would buy myself five days of peace by sending $1,000 a day.

Looking back now, I would say that we were good for each other and that the fire we went through together strengthened us both.

18
Breaking Through the Ad Barrier

Finally, by creative financing, PMA (Positive Mental Attitude) and JRT (Johnson Reinforcement Techniques), I bought enough time to identify and formulate the three elements necessary for a strategy of success.

The first element is identification of the problem. This is the most important point in developing a success strategy, and it's the one most frequently overlooked by business people from the mail room to the boardroom who leap into the saddle and ride off in all directions before they identify the objective and the obstacles.

That's the wrong approach. The first problem of any problem is to decide exactly what the problem is.

I didn't have a big staff and I didn't have a big bank account. The thing that saved me and Johnson Publishing Company is that I made the right diagnosis. I had to do what every businessman in a tight corner should do. I sat down and wrote a declarative sentence that defined the problem.

My problem was not the editorial content of the magazine—the readers were yelling for more. My problem was not circulation—I couldn't print enough copies. My problem was advertising or, to come right out with it, the lack of advertising.

How did I intend to deal with the problem?

I intended to deal with the problem by persuading corporations and advertising executives to give *Ebony* the same consideration they gave *Life* and *Look*.

To do that I had to convince corporations and advertising executives that there was an untapped, underdeveloped Black consumer market larger and more affluent than some of the major White foreign markets.

This was a revolutionary approach—revolutionary from a racial, marketing, and advertising standpoint—and I couldn't sell it to lower-level functionaries. I had to go to the top and sell the Black consumer market the same way you sell a foreign market.

The plan of action was implicit in the definition of the problem.

I needed, first of all, a team of advertising specialists who understood the new concept and believed in it with the passion of true believers.

The team didn't exist.

I had to invent it. I started, as usual, small. A small step gives you the confidence to make a big step. And a big step gives you courage to run.

I started by hiring a White advertising manager, a man named Irwin J. Stein, one of the most honorable men I've ever known. There were no Blacks who knew the mysteries of the White advertising world, and I hired Stein with the understanding that he would train a Black to take his place.

Stein wasn't a salesman; he was a manager. He helped design the rate cards and worked with me in determining rates. He also trained Isaac Payne, who succeeded him as advertising production manager and remained with the company until his death.

Since we didn't have a staff of salesmen, we asked a Black-owned firm of publishers' representatives to sell ads and look out for our interests on Madison Avenue. When our self-imposed advertising moratorium ended in May 1946, two of the first four ads in *Ebony* (Chesterfield, Kotex) were sold by this firm. I sold the other ads, Murray's Hair Pomade and Supreme Liberty Life Insurance Company.

The Chesterfield, Kotex, and Murray's ads were full-page color ads, and the Supreme ad was a full-page black-and-white. Murray's used a Black woman model. Chesterfield, which ran several ads in 1946 and 1947, used a White male model, and Kotex used a White couple.

When, after a few months, the Black firm did not seem to be making substantial progress, I turned reluctantly to a White firm. I was told that Whites could get in to see White advertising managers more easily and could socialize with them and promote the magazine better.

It didn't turn out that way. White salesmen were no more

effective than Black salesmen, and they created other problems. The turning point came on the day I got a call from an angry man in an advertising agency.

"John Johnson," he said, "I don't know whether I'm ever going to advertise with you, but I want to give you some free advice. You send a White man to sell me an ad for a magazine about Black people. This White man doesn't know any more about Blacks than I do. If you've got all those intelligent, affluent Blacks reading the magazine, why don't you send one to sell me an ad?"

It was a good question, and I decided, after thinking about it for a while, to send myself. What did I have to lose? I had tried everything, or almost everything, and I was floundering in a rough sea and going down for the third time.

From that day in 1946 until we turned the corner a year later, I spent almost every waking hour selling advertising.

Ebony readers helped. They jumped the gun and started asking manufacturers why they weren't advertising in *Ebony*. Some went further and told backsliders that they were only going to spend their money with companies that showed them the elementary respect of asking for their business.

An avalanche of postcards and handwritten petitions prepared the ground, and I planted seeds with letters and phone calls to corporate chiefs and agency heads. It was hard getting through, but fighting for my life, I placed as many as four hundred telephone calls to the same CEO.

There's an art in talking to secretaries, and it should be taught at MBA schools. I taught myself, and soon became a master of the art of leaping over secretarial shields. I was so persistent, and so patient, that some secretaries either put me through or gave me helpful hints.

The secretary to Fairfax M. Cone of Foote, Cone & Belding advertising agency told me she couldn't make an appointment for anyone.

"But," she added, "I'll give you a tip. He doesn't like to fly. He goes to New York every Sunday afternoon on the *Twentieth Century Limited*. He has a couple of drinks in the bar, eats dinner, and goes to bed. If I were you, I would just happen to be on that train, and I would wander into the club car and strike up a conversation with him.

I caught the train and wandered into the club car. And I was delighted to find Fairfax Cone there. I talked to him on that Sunday and the next Sunday and the Sunday after that. I became a regular on the *Twentieth Century Limited*, and Fairfax Cone and I became good friends. He arranged for me to talk to executives at his agency, and I sold some accounts. Cone himself later made a movie for us on the importance of the Black consumer market.

I used another approach to overcome the barrier at Tatham and Laird, headed by Kenneth Laird. Ken and I were active in the Roundtable of Christians and Jews. We served together on a number of committees and were virtually inseparable during Brotherhood Week. But the brotherhood slogans never led to anything concrete. We didn't get any business from Ken's agency, and when one of our standard accounts moved to his agency, we lost it. I pointed this out to him one day at a committee meeting on brotherhood, and he bristled with indignation.

"We don't believe in anything like that around here," he said. "I'll check it out and let you talk to our key people."

I talked to his executives and discovered what I already knew. They weren't the stumbling block.

I went back to Ken and said, "Ken, I've finally found the person in your agency who's keeping us from getting business."

"Who?" he said. "Tell me who it is, and I'll fire him."

"Ken," I said, "it's you."

He denied it. But he was forced to reexamine his own attitudes and to come to grips with the fact that a corporation or agency necessarily reflects the attitudes of the chief executive. Before long, we started getting business from Tatham and Laird.

19
The Turning Point

Working alone on unplowed ground with no guidelines or precedents, I had to improvise and make snap decisions based on my reading of how far I could go and what the traffic would bear.

I won some victories, but my losses overshadowed my gains. When we celebrated our first anniversary in November 1946, the future of the company was still in doubt. We put up a brave front, announcing a new advertising guarantee of 400,000, but we weren't making enough money to pay our bills. And behind the scenes things were going from bad to worse.

It was at this point that I decided to start four or five mail-order businesses that would advertise with me and produce revenue to pay for the advertising I needed and couldn't get.

The first business, Beauty Star cosmetics, marketed several hair-care products, including Satene. Long before I had a daughter, I liked the name Linda, which was used in Linda Fashions, a mail-order business that sold dresses and clothes. I also sold vitamins, books (Negro Digest Book Shop), and Star Glow wigs.

These businesses, especially the hair-care business, gave me breathing room, and I returned to the advertising campaign with new enthusiasm. The 1946 campaign had focused primarily on advertising agencies. In 1947, the turning point of the advertising campaign, I decided to focus on companies, which tell advertising agencies what to do. And I decided to focus on companies with a big but unacknowledged stake in the Black community.

My first target was Zenith Radio Company. Almost all Blacks owned radios, and most of them were Zenith radios. My mother owned a Zenith, all the people I knew owned Zeniths. If a case could be made for anybody advertising in *Ebony*, a case could be made for Zenith.

The head of Zenith was a former Navy Commander, a hard-driving, brilliant executive who ran the company the same way he had run his ships. I wrote him and asked for an appointment to talk about Zenith's advertising stake in Black America. The commander answered immediately and said, "I received your letter, but I can't see you. I don't handle advertising."

He was still my best target, and I wasn't going to let him get by with that routine reply.

All right, I said to myself, he's the head of the company and he doesn't handle advertising. What does he handle?

The answer was clear. He handled policy, including, presumably, advertising policy. I wrote another letter asking him if I could come in and talk to him about his *policy* on advertising in the Black community.

"You're a very persistent young man," he said in his reply, adding:

"I'll see you, because I always want to sell more things to more people. But,"—and he emphasized these words—"*if you try to talk to me about advertising, if you try to talk to me about placing an ad in your publication, I will end the interview.*"

I'd won—and I'd lost.

I had an appointment to talk to a CEO who said I could talk to him about anything except the one thing I wanted to talk to him about.

That presented a new problem. What would we talk about?

I went to *Who's Who in America*, which told me that the commander was an Arctic explorer who'd visited the North Pole several years after it was first explored by Matthew Henson and Commodore Robert E. Peary.

I knew from my own research that Henson, who reached the North Pole forty-five minutes before Peary and who was the first human to set foot on the icy hub of the world, was Black, that he was living in Harlem, and that he had written a book about his experiences.

This was the opening I needed. I asked Allan Morrison, our New York editor, to find Henson and ask him to autograph a copy of his book to the commander.

It occurred to me at that point that Henson was good copy, and I pulled a story out of our July 1947 issue and inserted a four-page story on Matt Henson.

As it turned out, Commander McDonald was thinking along the same lines. The first thing he said to me when I walked into his office was, "You see those snowshoes there? They were given to me by Matthew Henson. He was a Black man and he was as good as any two White men I ever knew. What do you think about that?"

I told him that Henson was also my hero.

He invited me to sit down—I was awestruck by this huge office, the size of a small auditorium.

"You know," he said, "I've often wondered what happened to Matt. I liked him and considered him a friend. I heard that he was living in New York and that he has written a book. Do you know anything about that?"

"Yes," I said, "I just happen to have a copy with me, and he was kind enough to autograph it to you."

He leafed through the book, obviously pleased by the autograph. He then said challengingly, "You say you put out a Black magazine. It would seem to me that any Black magazine would have done a story on a guy like Matt."

I agreed with him and said I just happened to have a copy of the magazine that contained a story on the Black explorer.

He looked through the magazine, nodding his head up and down in approval.

I told him I started the magazine to highlight the achievements of men like Matthew Henson, who'd demonstrated that excellence would break down all barriers.

"You know," he said finally, using the banned word himself, "I don't see any reason why we shouldn't advertise in this magazine."

He pushed a button and in came his advertising manager who'd told me no a thousand times.

The advertising manager bowed at the waist and said, "Yes, Commander."

"Mackey," said the commander, "why aren't we advertising in *Ebony*?"

I thought to myself, "I've got Mackey now."

But Mackey was cool.

"We're considering it, Commander," he said.

"By George," the commander said, "we ought to do it."

"Of course, Commander," Mackey said.

This was the turning point in my advertising campaign. We'd run ads before from Chesterfield and other companies, but the Zenith contract was our first major advertising schedule. And it paved the way for other schedules.

After Mackey left, the commander said, "I like your magazine and your story. I'm going to call a few of my friends and I want you to go in and tell them the same story you've told me."

While I was sitting there, he called the chairmen of Swift Packing Company, Elgin Watch Company, Armour Food Company, and Quaker Oats.

"I have a young man here," he said, "who's putting out a magazine. I think it has great potential, and I want you to see him. I can't tell you what to do about it, but will you please see him?"

All agreed to see me, and all bought ads.

The commander died in 1958, but the company is still one of our most faithful advertisers. In a development he couldn't have anticipated, I was elected to the Zenith board in 1971, and I'm still a member.

By coincidence in this bright summer, I found and hired a brilliant advertising specialist who made similar breakthroughs on the East Coast. His name was William P. Grayson, and the decision to persuade him to leave his job at the Baltimore *Afro-American* and go to work for me in New York City as our eastern advertising manager was one of the most important decisions I've made as CEO of Johnson Publishing Company.

Grayson, who handled all advertising for the *Afro-American* chain, suffered a stroke a few years ago and is no longer active, but he was one of the giants of the advertising field. He was creative, determined, and daring. He had an art background, which meant that he knew how to prepare and make presentations. He was a prodigious reader of different publications, which meant that he knew what was going on in the world and could relate our advertising appeals to the particular problems of advertisers.

It is rare in our field to find great salesmen who are also great managers. Bill excelled in both areas. When he started work in 1947, we rented a small office at 55 West Forty-second Street. He and his secretary, Margo Hughes, who came with him from the *Afro-American*, created the foundations of the crucial East Coast staff.

The first year Grayson came we were billing less than $25,000 a year. When he retired in 1970, we were billing more than $15 million.

Men with his skills are rare in Black or White America. To get him I offered him more than I was making and a bigger office. It was worth it. After Bill joined the staff, advertising sales increased dramatically. In November 1947 we had to omit 4,600 lines of advertising because of lack of space. By that time, our second anniversary, we could announce with pride that *Ebony* had weathered the storm.

In the months that followed we went from strength to strength. In February 1948 we increased the magazine size to sixty-eight pages to accommodate the new pages of advertising. In June we reached a peak of forty-eight pages of advertising and noted that we had broken, in the past six months, major accounts at Pepsi-Cola, Colgate, Beech-Nut, Old Gold, Seagram, Remington Rand, Roma Wines, and Schenley. In December, we ran the first four-color ad ever to appear on the inside of a Negro publication. Among the new corporations advertising regularly by that time were Elgin Watch, Zenith Radio, MGM and Capitol Records.

All through this period, while the advertising campaign was developing, *Ebony* was locked in a life-and-death struggle with another Black magazine, *Our World*. The struggle between us was the old story of the tortoise and the hare. The magazine's owner, John P. Davis, was colorful and flamboyant, and I was quiet and steady. The tortoise won. Somebody had to win, for there were not enough advertisers or readers for both magazines.

I have often said jokingly that the fundamental difference between the two magazines was dramatized by the last issue of *Our World*, which had a story on fifty-eight ways to make a fruitcake. I maintained then, and I maintain now, that people don't want to know fifty-eight ways to make a fruitcake. What they want to know is the *one* good way to make a fruitcake.

When *Our World* went into bankruptcy, I bought their assets, including their photo files. They had some great photos. One of the magazine's photographers, Moneta Sleet, Jr., joined our staff and became the first Black photographer and the first Black male to win a Pulitzer Prize. He was cited for a dramatic photograph of Coretta Scott King holding her young daughter at the funeral of Martin Luther King, Jr.

I spent a lot of time in the late forties recruiting editorial talent.

One of my first discoveries was Era Bell Thompson, author of *American Daughter*. I went to her small apartment under the "El" at Sixty-third Street and South Parkway and persuaded her to join our staff. She told me that she knew nothing about Negroes.

"That's all right," I replied, "we'll teach you."

When she retired twenty-eight years later, she said, "I think I'm beginning to understand Negroes."

For thirteen years, Era Bell was co-managing editor of *Ebony* with Herbert Nipson, a writer-photographer who'd earned a master of fine arts degree from the Writers Workshop at the University of Iowa.

In March 1948, the company had close to one hundred full-time employees and more than four thousand independent distributors.

Here again we were forced to create something that hadn't existed before: a new stratum of Black magazine editors and photographers. We sought out authors and major writers, and we stole the best talent from Black newspapers.

Another interesting staff member was circulation manager J. Unis Pressley. Pressley was so light-skinned that he could pass for White, and we quickly made him our official White. When we traveled it was his duty to register for a suite in the best hotels and to order a meal for four or five. We would then go up the freight elevator, pretending that we worked at the hotel, eat a good meal, take a hot bath, sleep in a soft bed, and sneak down the freight elevator the next morning. When we traveled in the South, Pressley would go into White cafés and buy food for the whole group.

Traveling in this period was a nightmare for Blacks. No matter how much money you had or how many degrees you'd earned, you could never be certain that your hotel reservation would be accepted. I'll never forget the night Bill Grayson and I showed up at one of the top Washington hotels to claim our reservations. Without even looking, the clerk said, "Sorry, we can't find your reservations."

Grayson and I were exhausted, and we didn't know anybody in Washington. We decided to sit in the lobby until they "found" our reservations or until we were arrested and taken to a cell where we could get a good night's sleep.

As it happened, the Daughters of the American Revolution were meeting at the hotel. When these little old ladies, many of them from the South, came out and saw two Black men sitting in the lobby, they started screaming and hollering, "Eek! Eek!" and running for cover.

"All right, fellows," the manager said. "You win. I found your reservations, but I want you to know, I will never, *never* find them again."

That experience is still alive within me, like an open wound. And I will sleep anywhere in Washington today, even on the ground—but not at that hotel.

Black frequent travelers knew one another. Almost all northern hotels had special floors or special sections on special floors—generally the fourth, fifth, or sixth floors where they had the catering offices and the banquet offices—that were reserved for Blacks.

There were similar problems in fancy nightclubs. Sammy Davis, Jr. and other Black headliners went to bat for us and forced clubs to seat us in special sections. At Chicago's famous Chez Paree, the Black side was always on the right side of the stage.

While we were fighting these battles, the world continued to turn. Jackie Robinson integrated baseball, Charles ("Chuck") Cooper integrated basketball, Kenny Washington integrated football, Ralph Bunche got a Nobel Prize for negotiating a settlement in Palestine, Harry Truman integrated the armed forces, and a federal court struck down segregation in D.C., prompting an *Afro-American* headline that I wish I had run: "Eat Anywhere."

Most of this progress was a product of impersonal forces, like the Cold War, but some of it was pressured by men like Adam Clayton Powell, the new congressman from Harlem; Walter White, the blond and blue-eyed black who headed the NAACP; and Asa Philip Randolph, who launched the March on Washington Movement.

Walter White, who was perhaps our first celebrity leader, was the de facto president of Black America. Whenever anything happened to a Black anywhere, even in Europe, Walter fired off a telegram and demanded action.

He was a charming man, probably the most charming man we've had in public life, and he called everybody by his or her first name. I remember that we waited with anticipation to see how Walter would address President Roosevelt's wife. We should have known. He treated her the same way he treated all Americans, Black and White. He called her Eleanor.

There was also a lot of discussion about Paul Robeson, who set a new record for Shakespearean drama on Broadway with his 296 performances in *Othello*. He was a persuasive symbol to Black men and women of all stations and situations. He was tall, handsome, with a deep booming voice and a dazzling smile. I don't think I've ever seen a more impressive man.

I thought to myself: Here's a man who has made it. A world figure. Phi Beta Kappa. All-American Singer. Actor. Scholar. Why doesn't he just enjoy his success and live a quiet life?

As if in answer to my unspoken question, he told us at a party one night that no Black would ever be truly free until all Blacks were free. He said that although he was a celebrated figure, he made it a practice never to go anywhere as Paul Robeson that he couldn't go as a Black man.

"None of us," he concluded, "can be satisfied with our little personal successes. Having made it ourselves, we must find our own particular way, depending on our education and profession, to give something back to the community and to those who are less fortunate than we are."

21
Going First Class

For as long as I can remember, I've been fascinated by the idea of going first class. That idea, which has nothing at all to do with money, is part of my management style. It's part of my operating philosophy. It informs my view of men, women, events, and the world.

From my standpoint, going first class is only a rough approximation of a meaning that transcends meaning. For, as Fats Waller told the woman who asked for a definition of jazz, "If you've got to ask, you'll never know."

Going first class means, among other things, going with class *and* style. There are people who have class but who don't have style. There are people who have style but don't have class. Going first class is going with class, style, grace, elegance, and excellence.

It's impossible to define the concept with mathematical precision. But most people know it when they see it.

There's first-class wine, and second-class wine.

There's first-class work, and second-class work.

For as long as I can remember I've been fascinated by the concept. This goes back, I think, to my childhood in the second-class section of Arkansas City and my days on welfare in Chicago and the years of being turned away from first-class hotels and restaurants.

I decided in those years that if I ever, *ever* had a chance to go first class I was never going second class again. I've held to that view. It's my personal policy, a policy born of experience, that Johnson Publishing Company goes first class or we don't go at all.

That policy came to the fore in 1949 when I wanted to move downtown. I was tired of working on back streets. South State Street was a back street. Calumet Avenue was a back street. I wanted to work on a front street. I wanted to go first class.

This was a tall order for a Black in 1949, and Eunice and I looked all over the South Loop for a two- or three-story building. One day she rushed into my office and told me that the old Hursen Funeral Home at 1820 South Michigan Avenue was for sale. I was delighted. Michigan Avenue was one of Chicago's great streets and 1820 was only eighteen blocks from the center of the Loop.

I called and asked Hursen the price of the building. He said $52,000. I asked if I could come by and see it. He said, "of course, what's the name of your company?"

"Negro Digest Publishing Company."

Silence. A long silence.

Then Hursen said he had a previous commitment and couldn't show the building to me then or later. There was a problem, in fact, and the building was no longer for sale.

I knew what the problem was. But it was useless to argue over the phone. Eunice and I found a White lawyer, Louis Wilson, who told Hursen that he represented a publishing house in the East and that he was sorry to hear that the building was no longer for sale. Hursen told Wilson that he had been misinformed. The building was still for sale. And the price of $52,000 was negotiable.

Wilson told Hursen that the eastern publisher was not interested in haggling, that he wanted to move in right away.

"There is, however, one stipulation. The people out East will have a Black man living on the place, as a kind of custodian, janitor, and bodyguard. Since they can't come out here, they want him to see the place and tell them what he thinks."

The arrangements were made, and I put on work clothes and followed Hursen around the building. He gave special attention to the boiler room that I would have to fire, he said, and the quarters on the top floor, where I would probably be living.

I told him, at the end of the tour, that I was impressed and that I was going to report favorably to my boss. Which I did, since I was the boss. The building was bought in trust so no one could identify the purchaser.

We paid $52,000 cash for the building—the money came from the sale of Beauty Star hair products—and spent $200,000 renovating it. When our friend, interior decorator Viola Marshall, got through with the old funeral home, it was one of the most elegant office buildings in Black America. "Decor in the roomy, three-floor building is sleekly modern," *Newsweek* said.

On Wednesday, June 1, 1949, we opened the new building with a champagne party that marked the real beginning of the *Ebony* success story. There were Black and White media executives, Black and White businessmen, and so many authors, artists and politicians that it was difficult to keep count. I was thirty-one on the night of my coming-out party, and I was a millionaire—seven years after I started *Negro Digest* with a $500 loan and a bootstrap.

There were stories on the *Ebony* miracle in media all over America. But few people knew my name. And nobody, or almost nobody, knew the man behind the name. Some said I was White. Others said I was a nonentity front for Whites. Still others said I didn't exist.

Some people, betraying their ignorance and their bias, said the magazine was so slick and professional and our offices were so elegant and functional that the owner couldn't possibly be a Black man. There were others who pointed to our White employees and said that if Whites didn't own it they soon would. It was widely said that our highly visible White executive editor was going to take the magazine away from me.

I was flabbergasted by this talk, which indicated, at the least, a lack of confidence in Black entrepreneurial skill and a lack of information. No one could "take" the company from me. I tried to explain, but rumors—which are impervious to facts—continued. They became so widespread that we took the extraordinary step of printing my photograph over a story which said, in effect, that this is John H. Johnson and he is a Negro.

The story in the "Backstage" section of the January 1947 *Ebony* said that I owned 100 percent of the stock along with my wife and mother.

"Johnson," it added, "is a Negro, as anyone with eyes can see....He is the brains and money behind this enterprise...."

This didn't end the rumors, which continued until *Life* folded and *Ebony* survived.

I ignored the rumors and dug in for the next phase of the *Ebony* journey. I was a success, by the world's reckoning, but I was a long way from home. I felt a sense of achievement, of exhilaration even, but I was still running scared. I was only sixteen years from the Mississippi mud, only thirteen years from welfare, and it was impossible for me to feel secure. Even today, I don't feel secure. A person who comes up from poverty, up from segregation, up from outhouses, up from welfare and humiliation and nos, can never feel secure, no matter how high he rises. He can never forget where he came from.

The magazine had changed, my bank account had changed, but I hadn't changed. There was, however, a critical and disorienting change in the way the world organized itself around me. People who'd never noticed me before noticed me. Society people who'd never sent me invitations before sent me invitations. I seemed to have grown larger in the world. I seemed to occupy a new space.

I'd been down and now I was up. Up was better.

Ebony. Tan. Copper. Hue. Jet. These were the colors of my personal rainbow. In the wild and fruitful years following the opening of my new building, I used four of these words to christen new magazines that were designed to corner the color market.

The runaway success of *Ebony* had made me king of the mountain in the undiscovered Negro consumer market. But the kingdoms of the media world are fragile things, and I lived in constant fear that someone or some thing might overrun my position and push me back down the mountain.

To forestall this possibility, I tried to anticipate every change in the market. Whenever I found a White magazine with strong Black readership, I brought out a Black counter-part, using names which tried to capture the color black, which, in Black America, includes all colors—cream, chocolate, anthracite, plum, cafe au lait, and burning brown.

During the true-confessions period, I brought out two magazines, *Tan Confessions* and *Copper Romance*. When in 1951, the market shifted to pocket-sized magazines like *Look* magazine's *Quick*, I responded with *Hue,* a pocket-sized feature magazine, and *Jet,* a pocket-sized news magazine.

Tan, *Copper*, and *Hue* made money and passed away, having satisfied the transient needs that called them into exist-ence. But *Jet* was a magazine of a different color. Like *Ebony*, which survived the *Look* and *Life* models, *Jet* survived *Quick* and added a permanent dash of blackness to the American media rainbow.

The word "jet" was tailor-made for my purposes. A talking word that sounds its message, jet means on one level a very dark velvet-black. And it means on another level fast, as in the airplane. From these dictionary definitions, it is but one step, and not a long one at that, to the Black American definition of "a fast Black magazine."

The name came to me in a roundabout way. Walter

Winchell kept running items saying that this person or that person was going to put out a Negro magazine called *Jet*. This went on for several months when I had no interest in starting a small magazine. When the winds changed and I decided to put out a compact, easy-to-read magazine, "jet" was clearly the best word for what I wanted to say and do.

I investigated and discovered that the name had been registered by a company that put out magazines for airplane mechanics. While other people were talking to Walter Winchell, I acted, buying the name and publishing on Thursday, November 1, 1951, the first issue of *Jet* magazine.

The pocket-sized magazine (5¾ by 4 inches) sold for fifteen cents. Edna Robinson, who was the wife of former middle-weight champion Sugar Ray Robinson, and who was one of the most beautiful women in the world, was on the cover of the first magazine.

"In the world today," I said in the first issue, "everything is moving along at a faster clip. There is more news and far less time to read it. That's why we are introducing our new magazine, *JET*, to give Blacks everywhere a *weekly news magazine* in handy, pocket-sized form. Each week we will bring you complete news coverage on happenings among Negroes all over the U.S.—in entertainment, politics, sports, social events, as well as features on unusual personalities, places and events...."

The lead story in the sixty-eight-page magazine was on the quashing of the remaining indictments against two Negroes and two Whites accused of conspiracy in the anti-Negro riots in the White Chicago suburb of Cicero. There were two other major stories. One was on the snubbing of Josephine Baker by Manhattan's Stork Club. The other was on the U.S. Senate confirmation of Dr. Channing Tobias as a delegate to the United Nations.

The first issue of the new magazine sold out everywhere and became a collector's item. Within six months, we were selling 300,000 copies a week and the magazine was the largest Black news magazine in the world, a position it has held now for thirty-eight years. Even at that early date, it was the focus of whole-souled attention in Negro America, where it was affectionately known as "the Negro's Bible." When a character in one of Maya Angelou's plays was asked if she'd read about a certain event in the *New York Times* or *Time*, she said, "If it wasn't in *Jet,* it didn't happen."

The phenomenal growth of the magazine continued after we increased the size (to 7⅜ by 5¼ inches) and the price ($1.25 in 1989). Thirty-eight years after it was founded, *Jet* sells 900,000 copies a week and usually has a full complement of ads from major advertisers.

When I did it the first time with *Negro Digest*, they said it was a fluke. When I did it the second time with *Ebony*, they said I was lucky. When I struck black gold the third straight time with *Jet*, there was a barrage of media stories, and people started talking about "the Johnson magic."

Now it was time to do something I'd been dreading. Somebody said once that you have to cut off old branches for new buds to blossom. That's good advice in dealing with trees and bushes, but pruning institutions linked to you by the umbilical cords of your first hopes is like cutting off your own arms and legs.

Negro Digest was a classic case of the conflict between my heart and the balance sheet. It was my first magazine love, and it will always have a special place in my heart. But it had become clear that my new magazines, *Ebony* in particular, had destroyed the circulation foundation of *Negro Digest*.

The old magazine still had a fanatically loyal group of subscribers, but the parade of pictures had passed it by. I discontinued it in November 1951, the same month that *Jet* was born. I'd learned by that time something James Bond didn't learn until later, that spies and businessmen and survivors should never say never. I made that clear when we discontinued the magazine, saying that we were stopping it for the moment but that we might revive it in the future.

In discontinuing *Negro Digest*, I acted from strength, not weakness. I was discarding from a strong hand because I needed the time and space to focus on the major managerial tasks of the decade: refining the formula and building a strong foundation for the surviving magazines.

23
Looking for Front Streets

After assembling the best advertising and editorial staff in Black America, I started looking for branch office space in major cities.

The search was complicated by racial barriers and my personal requirements. I didn't want *any* office space. I wanted the best space available. And it had to be on a front street. For I believed then, and I believe now, that an address says something about an individual or a company. It's a way of saying that you represent quality.

This was, in part, an extension of the lessons I learned at Supreme Life from senior executives like Harry Pace and Earl B. Dickerson. They were men of quality. They wore the best clothes, lived in the best neighborhoods, drove the best cars. They taught me a lesson I've never forgotten, that quality is the hallmark of success.

I was also influenced by my early experiences on the other side of Front Street in Arkansas City. The name was accurate. Arkansas City's Front Street was the foremost street. It was at the center of the commercial and social life of the city.

The first office we rented in New York City was a compromise. The only downtown office space I could find was on West Forty-second Street, which was a kind of back street. When our lease expired, I went to the landlord and asked for space in one of his properties on Fifth Avenue.

He looked at me as if seeing me for the first time, and said: "Johnson, you're not ready for Fifth Avenue yet. When you're ready, I'll let you know."

Livid with anger, I went to see others and soon had an offer for space in the Chrysler building, but I was aiming higher, and we'd heard that space was available in Rockefeller Center directly across from the new Time-Life Building. We talked to the sales representative, and he said that they had checked our credit references and we didn't qualify.

"Well," I said, "we want a two-year lease. What if we give you all of the cash in advance? Would that meet your requirement? He had the decency to blush in shame.

"Look fellows," he said, dropping his head. "It's really not me. It's somebody higher up."

I knew a man who was as high as you can get in Rockefeller circles. I'd met Winthrop Rockefeller at an Urban League affair, and I got his number in Arkansas and called him. I told him I was trying to find office space in New York and I understood that space was available in Rockefeller Center.

"Johnny," he asked, "is there space there?"

"Yes."

"Do you have the money?"

"Yes."

"You got it!" he said.

"What do I do now?" I asked.

He said, "Do nothing, somebody will call you."

Within an hour, I got a call from the president of Rockefeller Center, who wanted to show it to me personally.

I leased the space, hired an interior decorator, and ended up with one of the best looking offices in Manhattan.

I called Winthrop Rockefeller and told him it was a pleasure doing business with people at the top. He said he was pleased that it had worked out and didn't ask for a quid pro quo, but he said, in passing, that his brother Nelson was thinking about running for governor of New York and that the family would appreciate it if I would make sure that he got fair treatment in my magazines. I said I would, and I did.

The problems I faced in New York City were not unique. I was confronted with higher barriers in Washington, D.C., and roughly the same in Los Angeles. In trying to get on Wilshire Boulevard, I followed the Johnson rule, taking what I could get while continuing the campaign for something better.

Thus, by a roundabout route, with many strange turnings, we completed the circuit of front streets. Was it worth it? Of course it was worth it. Quality, like virtue, is its own reward.

The Avenue of the Americas, Pennsylvania Avenue, Wilshire Boulevard—we were on front streets from sea to shining sea. The only remaining real estate task—a task of the seventies—was to find the road to downtown Chicago.

Building on new and secure foundations, we moved in the fifties to make *Ebony* and the Negro consumer market integral parts of the marketing and advertising agendas of corporate America.

To accomplish this, we had to make four points: (1) that Black consumers existed; (2) that they had disposable income; (3) that they bought brand-name products; (4) that they could and would buy additional products if they were appealed to directly and personally.

Simple points. Obvious points. Why did it take so long to make them? One reason was the invisibility of the obvious. Nothing, in fact, is harder to see than what stares us in the face. The Negro consumer market was so big, so obvious, and so critically important to the balance sheets of American Industries that advertising and marketing experts couldn't see the forest for the trees.

Another reason, of course, was race, and the myths that made foreign markets more visible and appealing than the invisible and more profitable Negro markets in the undiscovered countries of Negro communities a few blocks away.

We broke through the plate glass of invisibility by proving that Black consumers not only existed, but that they bought proportionately more brand-name products than White consumers. We proved, for example, that Blacks were buying proportionately, more premium Scotch and more big cars than their White counterparts.

How did agencies and corporations respond to all of this?

They refused to believe it, even when Black researchers proved it, even when White researchers proved it, even when the U.S. Census Bureau proved it.

We were forced, therefore, to wage an agency-by-agency struggle that was so hard that even today it hurts me to think about it.

By far the hardest industry to sell was the automobile

industry. We sent an advertising salesman to Detroit every week for ten years before we landed our first major account at Chrysler, followed a few years later by General Motors. And this was in the days before routine air travel. The salesman made the round trip on the train every week.

Another major advertiser, Campbell Soup, didn't advertise with us or any other Black medium. Eastern advertising director William P. Grayson said he spent seventeen years, six months, five days, two hours, and thirty minutes on that account. It was, he said, like the labor of Sisyphus, pushing large stones up hills only to see them roll down again. He'd spend years persuading an advertising manager, and just as he was making progress, the manager would be transferred and he would have to start over.

I had a similar experience in Chicago trying to sell Sears Roebuck. I spent years trying to persuade them to advertise in our magazines on the theory that sooner or later somebody would have a change of heart. Fortunately for me, James Button, who'd been working for Sears in Canada and who was not familiar with American racial barriers, was promoted to the Chicago office. I told him the same story I'd been pitching for years, and he gave us our first Sears ad.

The basic point of these cases is persistence. I refused to give up. I refused to take no for an answer, and I refused to let others take no for an answer.

25
Selling Anybody Anything in Five Minutes

If I know enough about people, and if I have enough time, I can sell anybody anything.

Even if I don't have enough time, I can open the door to a future sale.

In my early days as a salesman, I usually asked clients and prospects for only five minutes. I've been known, in fact, to ask for only two minutes.

Sometimes you can't tell your story in five minutes, but if you ask for five minutes, people are more inclined to give you an appointment. If you get your foot in the door and tell a good story, they'll probably let you finish, even if it takes thirty minutes or an hour. If, on the other hand, there's no interest in what you're saying, a minute is enough.

It was my custom in the early days to ask for five minutes and to take fifteen or twenty minutes by creative ad-libbing. I would make my presentation in about five minutes, then stand up as if I intended to go. This usually relaxed the client, and I would say, "There's one more point I want to make."

Then, two or three minutes later, I would say, "I'm really going now, but I want to make sure you understand this point."

As I was going through the door with my briefcase, just before I pulled the door shut, I would pause, like TV detective Peter Falk, and say, "I just want to leave this final thought with you."

What made this five-minute drill effective was not the five minutes the client could see, but the weeks and months of preparation that he couldn't see. For when the five-minute clock started ticking, I knew more about him—more about his interests, passions, hobbies, desires—than most members of his family.

Whether I had five or thirty-five minutes, I always based my presentation on three tried-and-tested rules:

1. Grab the client's attention in the first two or three

seconds with a fact or an emotional statement that hits him where he lives or does business.

2. Find the vulnerable spot. Everybody has something that will make him or her move or say yes. It may have nothing in the world to do with his or her business life. It may be a dream or a hope or a commitment to a person or a thing. Selling is finding the vulnerable point and pushing the yes button.

A remarkable example of this was reported by William Grayson, who discovered that a powerful advertising executive was a fan of Roy Campanella, the great Brooklyn Dodgers catcher. The executive and his son virtually lived in the old Ebbets Field and worshipped the homeplate ground Campanella walked on.

Grayson, who lived down the street from Campanella, asked the baseball star to autograph one of his home-run balls to the boy. The ball carried not only Campanella's name but the date he hit the home run. By coincidence, the advertising executive and his son had been in Ebbets Field on the day Campanella hit the home run. That sold the account. Nothing— neither statistics nor pretty graphs nor hundreds of telephone calls—was as powerful as an unexpectedly powerful gift to a loved one.

3. Find and emphasize common ground. You and the client may disagree on many things. You may like Jesse Jackson and he or she may dislike Jesse Jackson. You're not there to talk about what divides you. You're there to emphasize the values, hopes, and aspirations that bind you together. Successful selling is a matter of finding common ground, no matter how narrow it might be, on which you and your client can stand together.

That's true in selling and life, especially in the area of race relations, where both Blacks and Whites must make a special effort to emphasize the things that unite them.

Does this mean that you have to sacrifice your integrity? Certainly not. I've been selling on the edge for forty-seven years, and I don't think I've had to compromise my integrity. I've stooped in some cases to conquer, but I don't apologize for that—the conquering, I mean.

You don't have to compromise your integrity to sell. You simply have to find and emphasize the things that unite you instead of the things that divide you.

By these different methods, by persistence and ingenuity and gall, I established narrow but solid common ground that gave me room to maneuver. Although I found and pushed a lot of yes buttons, the struggle for a fair share of the advertising dollar continued, and continues.

In advertising, as in politics, you're no better than your last schedule or your last election. No matter how many accounts you've landed, no matter how many elections you've won, you always start a new campaign at ground zero. And you're always faced with the task of going on cold and proving to a new audience how good you are.

26
Upstairs at the White House

The first time I met a U.S. president, he was talking about how hard it is to stop smoking.

We were upstairs at the White House, and Dwight David Eisenhower was presiding over a stag dinner of ten or twelve business leaders.

I was the only Black and the only publisher. Val Washington, a prominent Black Republican leader, had put me on the invitation list.

I've been to the White House many times since then, but this was my first and last dinner upstairs in the private quarters of the president.

After dinner we sat around and chatted over coffee and after-dinner liqueurs. The setting, small, private, personal, was made to order for Eisenhower, a genuinely likable person, natural and gracious. He'd recently stopped smoking, and somebody asked if he would ever smoke again.

"I don't know whether I'll start again," he said, "but I know damn well that I'll never quit again—quitting is too damn hard."

The president complained, like most citizens, about high taxes. He was living then in New York State, and he said he was going to move to Pennsylvania, where taxes were lower. True to his word, he later bought a farm near Gettysburg.

Toward the end of the evening, he let it be known that he would not oppose a draft for a second term. I understood then why I had been invited. The Republicans didn't have much Black support, and *Ebony* was, by then, the most powerful communicator in Black America. From Ike on, every U.S. president communicated with me because *Ebony* communicated so well with Black Americans.

Eisenhower said little or nothing that night about the problems of government. There was a feeling in Black America that he was a decent man who never really understood civil rights and the plight of Black Americans. I came away from the dinner with the feeling that he was a generous man and a great soldier whose career had distanced him from the day-to-day problems of urban America.

The White House dinner was, in part, a national coming-out party for the real John H. Johnson, who'd deliberately remained in the background until the company was organized on a sound basis.

Now, as the gathering Civil Rights Movement gained steam and force, I emerged from the corporate shadows and accepted positions on the boards of Tuskegee Institute and the National Urban League.

I was ready to become more active, and the National Urban League board put me on the fringes of that world and reminded me of the words of my friend and mentor, Earl B. Dickerson, who told me once, "If you want to succeed in White America, you must let your mind roam beyond the ghetto, even if your body is forced to remain in the ghetto. You must reach out into the world and tap into the minds of the people who are running the country, so you will know how far you can go and what path to travel in order to get there."

27
Ebony Fashion Fair

No matter where I am or what I'm doing, I'm always looking for successful ideas.

I can be socializing at a party or a wedding, I can be listening to a presentation at a meeting or walking through a department store, or driving through a city. All the while, microsecond after microsecond, the radar of my mind is revolving, tracking people and the environment, looking for openings in the wall of success.

In the course of a year, people come to me with hundreds of ideas for making money. Most of the ideas are worthless, but now and then a word or suggestion breaks the beam of my sentinel system and bells start ringing everywhere.

Before the decade of the fifties ended, the Johnson radar locked in on two opportunities that extended my reach and potential.

The first opportunity was an investment that led to majority control of Supreme Life Insurance Company, where I'd started my career as an office boy. Although I was technically still on leave of absence from Supreme, I had little or no relationship with the company or its officers from 1943 to 1957. As a matter of fact, I don't believe I set foot in the company headquarters for ten or more years. There was no particular reason for this estrangement. But after the death of Harry Pace, I got the feeling that some of the company officers were not comfortable with me and my success.

Earl B. Dickerson changed that. After he was elected president, he called and said, "You ought to return to the company in some way. You're a young man, you got your start here. Supreme is a part of your business heritage—and there's no reason why you shouldn't be involved in some way."

It was a generous offer, and I accepted it with no particular agenda. At Dickerson's invitation, I bought one thousand shares of his stock for $30,000 and was elected to the board of directors. I gradually bought more and more stock from individuals and from the company. When the company ran into financial difficulties and needed a new infusion of capital, I invested about a million dollars. All told, I put approximately $2.5 million in the company and became the largest stockholder and finally, the controlling stockholder.

When, in 1974, I was elected chairman and CEO, I felt a great sense of personal and corporate satisfaction. For I've only had two jobs in my whole life—and I still have both of them. In the first company, I started as an office boy and became chairman. In the second company, I started as chairman and remain chairman.

Not everyone was pleased. One veteran employee, who'd been at Supreme when I was an office boy and who had not treated me kindly, quoted Fats Waller at the end of my first board meeting, "One never knows, do one."

The second opportunity of the late fifties was the Ebony Fashion Show, which came to me, like so many of my ventures, as a gift wrapped in a problem.

The problem was the scarcity of Black models. They were hard to find, as Ernestine Dent, the wife of President Albert Dent of Dillard University, discovered when she decided to organize a charity fashion show for Flint-Goodridge Hospital. After exhausting her resources, she called me in late June 1958 and asked if I could help her locate some Black models.

The only Black models I knew were the Chicago and New York models we used in our enterprises, and I was not about to send them to New Orleans. But—and bells started ringing—what would happen, I asked myself, if I organized and controlled a fashion show that would meet the needs outlined by Mrs. Dent while contributing to the different needs—the need for models, fashion statements, circulation dollars—of Johnson Publishing Company?

I had no idea then how I was going to do it or even if I could do it, but I said quickly, "Mrs. Dent, I can't recommend any models, but what would you think if I put on the fashion show for you?"

"Oh!" she said, "that would be wonderful. But what would you want out of it?"

Before she completed the question, I'd figured out in my mind the financing scheme that we're still using thirty-one years later. I couldn't in good conscience charge a charitable organization a fee, but each ticket could be priced to include the cost of a subscription to *Ebony*.

"There'll be no expense to your organization," I said. "I'll furnish the models and the clothes. All I want is the three-dollar *Ebony* subscription, which will go to the person buying the ticket. Everything you charge above that will be yours free and clear."

So ran the plan, and so went the execution.

Two thousand people paid six dollars a ticket to attend the first Ebony Fashion Show, which was directed by Freda DeKnight and was held in September 1958 at Booker T. Washington High School. Mrs. Dent and her organization cleared $6,000. My share was $6,000, but I'd spent at least $25,000 for clothes, models, and production expense. This, however, was a small price for an idea that grew into the world's largest traveling fashion show.

Almost before the first show ended, I started planning the second show. With the help of Mrs. Dent, who called friends in other cities who wanted to sponsor events for charity, we produced a total of ten shows in 1958. In succeeding years, we added new sponsors—local Urban Leagues, sororities, community centers, the NAACP and UNCF.

In the sixties, the Fashion Show, under the direction of Eunice Walker Johnson, became a national institution, carrying the latest fashions by French, Italian, and American designers to localities and people who'd never been exposed to high-fashion environments. Today's show is a year-round business that travels to 190 cities in America, England, Jamaica, Bermuda, the Bahamas, and Canada and produces more than 300,000 subscribers for *Ebony* and *Jet*. Since the first show, we have raised more than $25 million for charity.

The Ebony Fashion Show has also given Black America

and the world a new concept of the kind of clothes Black women can wear. Before the Ebony Fashion Show, people said Black women couldn't wear red or yellow or purple. The fashion show proved that Black women could wear any color they wanted to wear. One of our earliest and best models, Terri Springer—tall, beautiful, shapely, and jet black—used to sashay across stages in spectacular colors that defined "Black is beautiful" before the phrase was invented. Many well-known Blacks, notably Richard Roundtree of *Shaft*, actress Judy Pace, and model Pat Cleveland, started as Fashion Fair models.

Like *Ebony*, like *Jet*, the fashion show was a quality project from the beginning. Every year we went to the fashion capitals of the world—New York, Paris, Rome—and bought two or three of the best garments of the premier designers. We also highlighted the contributions of Black designers. The current show features not only the big names of New York, London and Paris but also promising young Black designers in Los Angeles, Chicago, Dallas, Houston, and Atlanta.

28

Days of Pain and Glory

Eunice and I were so busy in the beginning building a business that we felt we didn't have time to build a family. Then, when we wanted children, we couldn't have any.

We went from doctor to doctor, from specialist to specialist. There was nothing wrong with us physically. Maybe the timing was wrong. We checked into Mayo Clinic, where both of us went through endless testing. Same result. Same answer. There was nothing wrong with us physically.

I know now that this happens to many couples. Sometimes a couple will adopt a child and then, through the birth process, produce three or four natural children. Sometimes the man and woman divorce, marry other partners, and both have housefuls of children.

This was not an option in our case. We were bound together by ties that were even greater than the desire to have children, and so we discussed the alternative of adopting children. This was an agonizing decision, primarily because of the myths surrounding parenthood. Men sometimes feel diminished if they don't have children, and some women feel alienated if they don't give birth to children. We discussed these and other attitudes and decided that a conscious and deliberate decision to adopt a child can be as fulfilling and transforming—for the child and the parents—as natural childbirth.

Having made this decision, we went to an Illinois adoption agency which investigated us for almost a year. I was a little surprised by this scrutiny, for I thought, in my innocence, that it was obvious that I was qualified for parenthood. But agency officials seemed to know what they were doing. They were interested in compatibility. They wanted to match the child to the parents and the parents to the child.

After an interminable wait, the big day came, and we took our two-week-old son home in June 1956. There was not a moment's doubt or hesitation about the name. Even before we

saw him, we knew that he was—what else?—John Harold
Johnson, Jr.

You can climb Mount Everest or make a million dollars or
dine at the White House, but there's nothing like the joy and
terror of parenthood. I shall always be grateful to John Harold
for that lesson. He hadn't been in our home for a week when I
realized that being a parent is not so much giving birth as
giving love and attention and sleepless nights.

From the beginning, John was a night person, who cried all
night and slept all day. Eunice and I took turns walking the
floor, but we were so proud to have him that we never complained. We could have hired nurses or babysitters, but Eunice
wanted to do it herself. We had a housekeeper then, but the
housekeeper was responsible for the house, not the children.

Two years later, we went back to the same agency and
adopted a two-week-old girl and named her Linda Eunice.

Talk about happy. We were as happy as a family can be.

Until the trouble started. We noticed in the second year
that John developed colds he couldn't shake and fevers that
lasted longer than they should have. We took him to Dr. Edward Beasley, a dear friend, who hesitated and finally said he
had sickle-cell anemia.

Until that moment I'd never heard of sickle-cell anemia.

"What's that?" I asked.

It was, he said, a chronic hereditary blood disease that
occurs primarily among Africans or persons of African descent.
He went on to say a lot of big words I didn't understand about
abnormal hemoglobin causing red blood cells to sickle. But I
understood the end product: enlarged spleen, anemia, lethargy,
joint pain, blood clot formation, death.

"All right," I said, "what's the cure?"

"There is no cure," he said. "Most victims die before they
reach the age of thirty. I know this is sad news for you, but it's
the best I can tell you. The adoption agency should have tested
for sickle-cell before they gave the child to you."

I left Dr. Beasley's office in a daze, not knowing what to
do or where to go. I finally called the adoption agency and said,

"Miss, why didn't you give my son a test?"

"Well, you know," she said, "we really overlooked that. It's our fault and we'd be happy to take him back and give you another child."

I exploded, and it's hard even today for me to talk about it without breaking down.

"Lady," I told her, "you've got to be crazy! He's my son, he's been in my home for two years. I don't care what he has— I'm not giving him up. I'm just saying that you ought to do these tests for other people."

And so it began, periods of calm and happiness punctuated by periods of crisis and pain, when it seemed that John was going to die. As the months and then the years slipped by, the crisis periods got progressively worse and the periods between the crises became shorter.

Fortunately, we lived on Drexel Square, which was only five minutes from the University of Chicago, and my wife's brother, a doctor, lived nearby. We were very fortunate in this respect, for John had a severe case and probably wouldn't have lived ten years if he hadn't come into our home, which was blessed with good medical care and other resources.

John lived twenty-five years. I've said many times that I believe the Lord sent him to our home so we could prolong his life. We suffered most of those twenty-five years and were blessed in terms of what Gladys Knight called in her song, "the pain and glory"—because there was always pain, and yet there was always happiness and glory.

Family life and the problems surrounding John's illness changed my life and my perspective. I cut back on my traveling and tried to get home every night for dinner. Although I still went to the office on Saturday, I made a point of spending all day Sunday with Linda and John. We went to the zoo or we went riding, whatever they wanted to do. Sunday was their day. And Monday and Tuesday, too. For they were always in and out of the office, and they were always begging employees for nickels and dimes for the pop machine.

Linda, who was elegant and outgoing from the beginning,

developed a passionate interest in horseback riding and fashions. When she was only seven, she toured the fashion capitals of Europe with her mother. Since then she has been back to Europe at least fifty times.

John developed an early interest in photography, and shot several stories for *Ebony* and *Jet*, including one on skydiving that required so much daring that nobody else wanted to do it.

Looking back now, I think he knew his time span was limited and that he had a rendezvous with death. So he had no fear of death. He liked to race cars and to sky-dive and to ski. He liked to do dangerous things. That worried me a lot, but I never tried to stop him. I knew that he didn't have a lot of time and that he wanted to use the time he had to the fullest.

He was only eighteen when he got married. Nobody in the family was happy about the marriage, but nobody could tell him to wait, because we knew he didn't have the time. We gritted our teeth, smiled over our concerns, and gave the bride and bridegroom our best wishes. And that's the way it should have been, really.

Because of my experiences with John and Linda, I grew as a person and as a publisher. I had a greater awareness of the need for strong family units, and my interest in adoption was reflected in the number of stories *Ebony* did on families and adoptions.

29
Nkrumah, Haile Selassie, and the Kitchen Confrontation

Five, maybe six centuries after my ancestors were dragged in chains across the Atlantic, I went back to Africa with a vice president of the United States of America.

There was history and irony in this.

For Vice President Richard M. Nixon was the head of the integrated United States delegation to the Ghana Independence Ceremony that marked the beginning of the end of the colonial domination of Africa.

To record the event for posterity, and to gain international exposure for his predicted presidential race, Nixon asked a group of Black and White press people to accompany him.

Eunice and I were in the group that left Andrews Air Force Base in Washington and reversed the Atlantic crossing routes that brought millions of Africans to the New World.

Nixon went out of his way to make sure we received equal treatment. We started out with two airplanes, one for the press and one for the vice president. The press plane was an ancient affair which sputtered and smoked and made frequent stops for maintenance. The maintenance personnel told us that it was perfectly safe, but we didn't believe it until the vice president decided to ride on our plane to prove that it was.

The plane made it to Accra, Ghana, where on midnight, March 6, 1957, the Union Jack was lowered and the Ghana flag was raised. This set off a paroxysm of cheering and weeping. It was not entirely clear where all this was heading, but one thing was obvious: the old world of colonialism was dead, gone forever. Strangers, Black and White, hugged, kissed, and cried. The people of Ghana danced in the streets all night long.

This was my first visit to the land of my fathers and mothers. For the first time, I saw Black men in charge, running the country. I saw a Black supreme court justice, a Black attorney general. I saw Black people in authority, heads held high in confidence and strength.

This gave the large African-American contingent a lift. It gave us a new spirit and new energy to come back home and deal with the remaining obstacles to the Dream. "We Africans," a Ghanaian told me, "have our freedom. When are you Negroes going to get yours?" We got the message and returned to America, determined to get ours.

I was impressed by Kwame Nkrumah, who was both a dreamer and a realist. He spoke that week of his dream of a United States of Africa. He may have been right in stressing the potential of a union of African states, but he tried to move too far too soon, and destroyed himself.

Despite all that, his place in history is secure. He gave us pride in our being and confidence in our destiny. He was the first fruit, to paraphrase W. E. B. DuBois's eulogy to Marcus Garvey, of a mighty coming thing in Africa, in the Caribbean, and the little Africas of North and South America.

I had a long conversation with Nkrumah, (who was not called Showboy for nothing), at one of the special events. He'd been trained in America at Lincoln University (Pa.) and said, "I owe a debt of gratitude to the Black people of America. As a student there, I went to NAACP meetings, read about your struggles in Black newspapers and was inspired. I was tempted to stay and live an easier life, but the struggle of American Negroes inspired me to come back and fight harder for my people."

During this trip I met Martin Luther King, Jr. for the first time. I'd talked to him several times on the telephone, but we'd never met. I saw him across a crowded room at the Government House ceremony. I recognized him immediately, and he recognized me. Before I could reach him, he pushed through the crowd and pumped my hand, thanking me for the coverage and support. "Brother Johnson," he said in that rich and unforgettable baritone, "I'll always be grateful."

I left Ghana with mixed emotions. It was clear then that the British had given the Africans political power but had kept the economic power. They kept the banks, they kept the insurance companies and the factories and the money. It was like giving someone a Rolls-Royce without a motor.

As a result, the Ghanaians found themselves on the morning after in a no-win situation. I've thought many times since then of the similarities between the transfer of power in Africa and the transfer of power in the big cities of America. For political emancipation is provisional and ultimately meaningless if it is not followed by economic emancipation. The best of the big-city Black mayors, Harold Washington and Maynard Jackson in particular, understood that. They moved immediately to buttress political ballots with the economic ballots of set-asides. They also created concrete guidelines that gave Blacks, Hispanics, and women a piece of the economic as well as political action.

We could see this imperative clearly as we followed the vice president on a tour that included seven additional African countries, including Liberia, which had been founded by descendants of American slaves but was still mired in economic difficulties.

The highlight of our tour was a visit to Ethiopia, one of the world's oldest countries. The country was ruled by the legendary Haile Selassie, the Conquering Lion of Judah. When we arrived at his palace, White reporters and officials pushed their way to the front, obscuring our view of the emperor, who sat on a throne, flanked by two lions. The lions, I noted with concern, were held securely by two huge men. The emperor was a small man, but he held himself erect and seemed to be six feet tall.

When the audience began, the emperor rose, looked out over the crowd, and said, "Where is the man from *Ebony*?"

There was a stir among his aides and he said again, "Where is the man from *Ebony*?" I held up my hand in the back, and Security ushered me up to the throne. The emperor congratulated me on the job *Ebony* was doing in letting the people of the world know about the progress of American Blacks. He said he was an avid reader of *Ebony*, but that he was having trouble with his subscription. I told him that I would take care of it. We'd been sending his magazines directly to

Ethiopia, and they were oftentimes delayed, lost, or even stolen. An aide told me to send the magazine to the Washington embassy so it could go by diplomatic pouch to the emperor.

In 1959, Eunice and I were among the media representatives who went with Vice President Nixon to Poland and Russia. It was on this trip that Nixon had his celebrated confrontation with Nikita Khrushchev in a kitchen at the American Pavilion of the World's Fair.

Eunice and I were standing in the dining room when the confrontation began. And we were astonished when Nixon and Khrushchev started pointing fingers at each other and talking excitedly. The story has been told many times, but I've never read an account that conveyed the sense of menace we felt. I thought, "We'll never get out of here alive." But they were both politicians, and they realized that this was a great stage, a world stage, on which to continue the Cold War struggle.

Despite the tensions of the time, I was treated courteously by the Russian people. It was a little disconcerting, however, to deal with the hundreds of Russian children who followed me around and tried to feel my hand to see if the black would rub off.

One of the fascinating sidelights of the trip was related later by Ralph McGill, the publisher and editor of the *Atlanta Constitution*. McGill noted that Eunice and I were members of the press party and added:

> We had become friends and had many talks. At Sverdlovsk (where Francis Gary Powers and his U-2 plane not long thereafter were to meet disaster) the Soviet journalists invited the visiting press corps to dinner—with dancing. The day had been long, hot and exhausting, and we sat gratefully down to a good dinner....
>
> One of the Russian-speaking U.S. staff members sought me out and said, "I thought you might like to know that I have heard the Soviet newsmen talking. They are waiting to see if you, from the South about which they have heard so much and know so little, will ask Mrs. Johnson to dance? If you do, they won't mention it in their dispatches. If you don't it may well be

a featured part of the news from here."

So I sought out Mrs. Johnson. "Mrs. Johnson," I said, "I haven't danced in perhaps twenty years. I was never any good at it and, with general approval, gave it up. But I think we must dance for the honor of our country." I then told her the story. "I am exhausted," she said, "and my feet are, as the saying goes, killing me. But we mustn't disappoint them." So, later when the music began, I went to Mrs. Johnson and asked if she would dance. She would. Indeed, we were the first on the floor. There was no feature story from Sverdlovsk that night.

We spent a lot of time with Nixon in press conferences and briefings. When we returned to America, Nixon, who was running hard for president, invited us to his home. I noticed with delight that both *Ebony* and *Jet* were prominently displayed on his magazine shelf, along with other major magazines. One of the reporters said, "You know he did it for this occasion." I replied, "I don't care why he did it, he did it." Nixon later sent a scroll which made us members of his Kitchen Cabinet.

30

New Frontier with the Kennedys

The sixties were the most exciting years of my life.

During these magical ten years, Black Americans made their greatest gains, and millions of Whites, especially White women, White students, and the White elderly, profited from a struggle that changed everything—politics, education, religion, sex.

I was forty-two when the decade began. When it ended ten years and ten revolutions later, I was fifty-two and a new and different person.

In the intervening years, *Ebony* made its greatest circulation gains, moving from 623,000 in 1960 to 1,217,000 in 1970. During the same decade, I received extensive national recognition and became for the first time well known outside my own profession.

As the editor and publisher of America's biggest Black magazine, and as a businessman with access to the leaders of corporate America, I had a unique appreciation of the events and people who made these years unforgettable.

I was drawn into the presidential campaign that foreshadowed the coming struggles. Senator Kennedy wanted me to come to Washington for a meeting in his office.

I declined, citing the pressure of business. But that wasn't the real reason. I'd just returned to America after a trip to Africa with the press contingent accompanying Nixon. Although I was not a Republican or supporter of Nixon, I did know him.

Senator Kennedy was an unknown quantity. He had a way with words, and he had dash and style. But some people thought he was a rich playboy with little or no understanding of Black America.

The senator came back with a new proposal. "What," he asked, "if the Kennedys extend a social invitation—will you come to Washington then?"

"Well," I said, "if I get an invitation, I'll consider it."

Eunice and I went to Washington and stopped by the Georgetown home of Senator and Mrs. Kennedy for a relaxed and delightful supper. The Kennedys' daughter, Caroline, sat in a baby chair by the table as we ate.

The main reason Senator Kennedy wanted to see me was to express concern about coverage in *Jet*. He mentioned specifically stories which said he didn't have a Black secretary in his Washington office. The stories neglected to mention that he did have a Black secretary in his Boston office and that Nixon didn't have a Black secretary anywhere.

I agreed with him and told him I would see that he got fair coverage in *Jet*.

"I'm glad you're fair-minded," he said pulling his chair closer. "Now that you're going to do this for me, what can I do for you? You know, I'm going to be president. Would you like to be an ambassador? Would you like a high government post? What do you want? I believe in paying my political debts."

"Gee, Senator," I replied. "I really don't want any of those things. I'm trying to succeed as a publisher, and I have no other ambition. I understand your father is active in the liquor business. Maybe you could speak to him and he could pass the word around so I could get some advertisers, which I really need."

He said he didn't know if he could do that. "But let me see what I can do."

Less than a month later, my secretary told me Henry Ford II was on the line.

"Mr. Johnson," he said, "I was up at Hyannis Port with Senator Kennedy last week. He told me you're a fine young man who puts out a good magazine. He asked if I would consider giving you some advertising. I'm calling to tell you that we're going to, and I want you to know that I'm doing it because of Senator Kennedy."

So, after an advertising campaign of at least ten years, we got our first Ford ad.

After the 1960 election, Kennedy broke new ground,

carrying Blacks and Whites across many frontiers. For the first time, large numbers of Blacks attended the inauguration of a president and danced and sipped champagne at the social events.

I took my mother and stepfather and my wife's mother and father to the 1961 inauguration. For Eunice and me, it was the opening of a new door in history. For our parents and for members of their generation, it was a social and political miracle.

This was a new and heady experience for Blacks and Whites, who began the still uncompleted task of dealing with each other openly and frankly as Americans.

The Kennedys never missed a trick. On Tuesday, July 25, 1961, I went to a stag luncheon at the White House for Nigerian Prime Minister Abubakar Tafawa Balewa. After the luncheon, I flew back to Chicago. When I landed at O'Hare, there was an urgent message from the White House. Airport officials rushed me to a phone—the president wanted me to represent the United States at the Independence Ceremony of the Ivory Coast. The four-man delegation was to be headed by the president's brother, Attorney General Robert F. Kennedy, and I was to hold the rank of special ambassador.

Within days, I was en route to the Ivory Coast on a presidential plane with Robert and Ethel Kennedy and G. Mennen Williams, the assistant secretary of state for African affairs. The fourth member of the delegation was Ivory Coast Ambassador R. Borden Reams.

Just before one of the major events of the Independence Ceremony, Ambassador Reams came to me with a surprising story.

"John," he said, "I was only able to get four tickets to this affair. We could give the tickets to Mr. and Mrs. Kennedy and Mr. and Mrs. Williams, and I would find something for you and me to do."

This seemed strange. I was the only Black on an official delegation to the Independence Ceremony of a Black country, and the ambassador was saying he didn't think I should attend a major event. When he asked what I thought, I told him I was not the head of the delegation, and it was a matter for Mr. Kennedy to decide.

He hiked down the steps, and I hiked down behind him to eavesdrop on what was being said. He told the same story to Robert Kennedy, who thought for a moment and said: "First of all, Ethel and I need two tickets. And John Johnson, of course, will need one—I don't care what you do with the other one."

The ambassador, who had only one ticket for his immediate boss and his wife, turned two or three colors, ran all the way to the palace, and came back with the proper number of tickets. We never had that problem again, and Bobby Kennedy never mentioned it to me.

From that moment on, he was one of my favorite people.

When the Ivory Coast president, Felix Houphouet-Boigny, came to America, Eunice and I attended the White House dinner, hosted by the president, and the Blair House dinner hosted by the African president.

Tragedy and struggle changed both President Kennedy and his brother. The changes were clear to me when I went to the White House with other Blacks to celebrate the one hundredth anniversary of the Emancipation Proclamation. The president I saw on that night wasn't the same man I'd met five years before in Georgetown.

The White House reception was on February 12, 1963. Five months later, after forcing the registration of two Black students at the University of Alabama, Kennedy made a speech that was one of the defining events of his presidency. In that speech, a U.S. president said for the first time that segregation was morally wrong.

"One hundred years of delay," he said, "have passed since President Lincoln freed the slaves, yet their heirs, their grandsons, are not fully free. They are not free from the bonds of injustice; they are not yet free from social and economic oppression. And this nation, for all its hopes and all its boast, will not be fully free until all its citizens are free."

The next day, Wednesday, June 12, a segregationist added

an exclamation point to this speech by assassinating Medgar Evers in front of his Jackson, Mississippi home.

Like almost all Americans, Black and White, I was alternately elated and enraged by these events. And I was one of the 250,000 Americans, Black and White, who climbed the heights with Martin Luther King, Jr. in the March on Washington.

I'd never witnessed a day like that before, and I'm sure I'll never see one like it again. Black and White together, celebrity, labor unionist, and entrepreneur together. And people from everywhere—Josephine Baker from Paris, Marlon Brando and Sammy Davis, Jr. from Hollywood, priests, nuns, sinners, all united in one of the greatest demonstrations for freedom in our history.

I mobilized a small army to cover the event. We have more photographs from that event in our files today than any other medium or organization.

In September, I had a private meeting with the president, who talked about race relations with a new sense of urgency and maturity. He congratulated me on our Emancipation Proclamation Centennial edition, and we posed, holding a copy of the famous cover of Frederick Douglass.

The next month, in October, Kennedy named me to the official delegation for the Independence Ceremony of Kenya, with the rank of special ambassador.

A month later, he was dead, gunned down in Dallas.

Horrified like almost all Americans, I tried to make some sense out of the whirlwind of events. After my appointment was reconfirmed by President Johnson, I went to the Kenya celebration in December 1963, convinced that freedom was on trial not only in Africa but also in America.

31

Special Ambassador to White America

In the decade of the long hot summers, I held the unofficial position of special ambassador to American Whites.

As city after city erupted in riots, I was forced by circumstances and my unique vantage point on the Black and White watchtower to assume the role of interpreting Black America to corporate America and corporate America to Black America.

I made at least two hundred speeches during this period to business leaders stunned by the revolution of rising expectations.

I tried not to be self-serving in my response to White corporate leaders, who were astonished and dismayed by the depth of Black feeling.

Whether in speeches or in one-on-one encounters, I emphasized fair employment and equal opportunity, pointing out that it was the responsibility of the CEO to ensure that his managers carried out his policies.

I called for larger contributions to Black educational institutions and asked corporate leaders to assume personal responsibility.

Enlightened self-interest: that was my theme. I asked corporate leaders to act not for Blacks, not for civil rights, but for their corporations and themselves. For it was true then and it's true now that if you increase the income of Blacks and Hispanics and poor Whites, you increase the profits of corporate America. And if you decrease the income of the disadvantaged, you decrease the income and the potential income of American corporations.

"What we have to deal with today," I said, "is a major shift in the mood of Negro people. The New Negro Consumer is demanding full participation in the American marketplace and insists that businessmen deal with him as an American and as a human being. Integration of the Negro into the American Common Market would be the equivalent of adding a whole new nation of producers and consumers."

"Negro Americans," I said, "are in the streets demonstrating and protesting. You can't service your clients adequately if you don't know why they are in the streets....No one who watched the acres of people in the March on Washington—as I did—can say that he doesn't understand the depth of the Negro's discontent."

It was a crucial turning point in the relations between Black and White Americans. It all boiled down to the fact that equal opportunity was good business.

Lyndon Baines Johnson, the first southern-based president since Andrew Johnson, hadn't been in office for a month when I started getting indirect messages from the White House. Whitney Young told me the president called him in the middle of the night and asked, "Whitney, why don't they like me at *Jet*?" Other leaders received similar calls.

One day about five o'clock in the afternoon, Carl Rowan called and said the president wanted to see me right away. I told him I would come the next morning.

When I arrived, I was ushered into the Oval Office for one of the happenings of the sixties, a one-on-one with Johnson. As soon as I crossed the threshold, the president started talking, telling me what he had done and was doing for Black people and that he didn't see why *Jet* was always criticizing his administration and picking at this and that. It was tragic, he said. It was getting in the way of the progress he was trying to create for Blacks and playing into the hands of those no-good bleep bleep bleeps who hated Lyndon Johnson and Negroes. He went on like this for about thirty minutes without giving me a chance to say one word, and most of the words he used about his critics couldn't be printed.

When he paused for a breath, I said, "Well, Mr. President, what do you want me to do about it?"

He said, "I want it stopped."

I said, "It's stopped."

He paused, stunned. "Just like that?"

I said, "Just like that." I told him I'd reviewed the stories and that some of them were obviously unfair. The problem was that our people were Kennedy people who resented the fact that Kennedy was dead and that somebody was trying to take his place. So I told him I would make sure that he got fair coverage in our magazines.

"Well," he said, "now that that's over, why don't you and I pose with a copy of *Jet*."

I said, "Gee, Mr. President, I don't have a copy of *Jet*."

He pulled a copy out of his pocket and said, "I just happen to have one."

And the photographer was called in to record two southerners, one Black, one White, holding up a copy of *Jet*.

What impressed me about President Johnson was his persuasiveness. If he hadn't committed himself to politics, he would have made a master salesman. He'd always pull his chair up close to you and talk to you in a soft voice, looking you straight in the eyes. He mesmerized the people he was trying to convince, and it was hard to say no to anything he asked.

After our first meeting, we became friends, and I was invited to the White House many times. At most dinners, I was seated next to President Johnson. When Thurgood Marshall was appointed solicitor general of the United States, I was sitting next to the president, and he said, "Now Mr. Johnson, I've just appointed Thurgood Marshall solicitor general. You're a bright young man, I don't have to tell you why I did that, do I?"

"Of course not, Mr. President," I replied. "I hope he succeeds and that you do what I think you're going to do." Which was to give Marshall experience at that level before appointing him to the Supreme Court.

Shortly afterward, I was seated at the president's table at a stag dinner. It was customary at these dinners to put names in a hat and pull out one name for each table. That person was supposed to get up and give the president some advice on how to run the country.

Whether by design or accident, my name was picked at my table. I sat there in a quandary because I knew that the last thing Johnson wanted was advice on how to run the country. When my turn came, I stood up and said, "My mother's name was Johnson, my wife's name is Johnson. I've never had luck giving advice to Johnsons—and I'm not going to start tonight."

The room exploded in laughter and applause. Nathan Pusey, the president of Harvard, sent me a little note, "You are ahead." When the last speaker finished, he sent me another note, "You're still ahead."

32

Black is Beautiful (and White, Too)

Between 1960 and 1970, Black America reinvented itself, changing both its color and its name. The name *Black* replaced *Negro* and *colored*. The color black replaced brown and even white in the center of the black spectrum. Black consciousness. Black love. Black fire. Black power. *Black World.*

This was perhaps the most significant and dangerous hairpin turn in Black history, and it created havoc in the offices of institutions for people who couldn't cope with sudden change.

Suddenly and dramatically, the walls came tumbling down almost everywhere. The number of Negroes in college doubled and tripled, and the Black middle class multiplied. There was, at the same time, a quantum jump in Black consciousness.

For the first time Blacks came into their own. They respected themselves as Black people whether they were very dark or very light or in between. Color, in fact, lost its importance. If there was an edge it was with the darker colors. But, after a period of friction, it finally settled down to the point where we were just Blacks without regard to shades or tints.

Johnson Publishing Company played a leadership role in this process on three levels. First, we helped create the foundations of this struggle in the forties and fifties when the ground was hard and there were few laborers. Secondly, we anticipated the changes and gave focus and form to them. In 1959, for example, we detected a growing interest in Black history and authorized a pathfinding Black history series. The response was so enthusiastic that we published a book, Lerone Bennett's *Before the Mayflower*, one of the most widely read Black history books ever. This marked the beginning of the Johnson Publishing Company Book Division.

We didn't follow the parade; we were out front, beating the drums and pointing the way. Our series on "Black Power" preceded the first call for "Black Power." We were the first major magazine to say that the race problem is also a White problem ("The White Problem in America").

We also spoke frankly to Black America, denouncing "Black on Black Crime" in a prize-winning special issue, and calling for community action to deal with teenage pregnancy and drugs.

I published these stories with reservations. There was no way to know then how advertisers or readers would react. Before the issue on "The White Problem" went to press, one of my editors asked, "Boss, do you know what you're doing?" I didn't know what I was doing, but I was preaching the virtues of "responsible daring" in the White community, and there was no alternative to "responsible daring" in the Black community.

On a third and equally important level, we changed with the changing times. We followed the consciousness of the times by defining success narrowly in terms of material things. We needed to know then that some Blacks were living as well as some Whites. But as the magazine matured and as Blacks changed, we broadened the formula for success, defining it as the achievement of a positive goal of whatever a person set out to do.

Winning a civil rights battle was success.

Raising a family was success.

Sending children to college was success.

Earning an MBA or making an outstanding professional contribution was success.

This changed the magazine. Before the sixties we were 50 percent orange juice and 50 percent castor oil. For most of the sixties we were practically all castor oil. Readers embraced the new formula. They hungered for it. They were more interested in being men and women than being entertained.

We must have been doing something right. My leading magazines reached all-time highs in the sixties, and we received unprecedented acclaim in the Black and White communities. When we celebrated the twentieth anniversary of *Ebony* in November 1965, *Ebony* was selling 900,000 copies a month, and its three sister magazines, *Jet*, *Tan*, and the revived *Negro Digest*, were selling a total of 2.3 million copies a month.

33
Celebrating on Two Continents

Ed Sullivan said it was "the greatest show going on anywhere in the world." Arthur Godfrey, Lena Horne, Duke Ellington, and Muhammad Ali agreed.

They were among the eight hundred CEOs, ad executives, and celebrities who filled the Starlight Roof of the Waldorf-Astoria on Monday, November 29, 1965, for the twentieth-anniversary celebration of *Ebony* magazine.

Never before had so many certified Black and White legends gathered under one roof. Among the guests were Roy Wilkins, Whitney Young, Thurgood Marshall, Robert C. Weaver, Dorothy Height, Sammy Davis, Jr., Cab Calloway, Ossie Davis, Carl Rowan, Frederick O'Neal, Louis Gossett, Brock Peters, Diana Sands, Langston Hughes, Jim Brown, Roy Campanella, and Jackie Robinson.

Clifford Alexander read a special greeting from President Johnson. Vice President Humphrey toasted *Ebony* in a moving ten-minute film.

"What a remarkable success story this is," he said. "Starting out in November 1945, as little more than a dream in Johnny Johnson's eye, *Ebony* today is a leader among national magazines. With a circulation which has grown to almost one million copies, the growth of *Ebony* parallels almost precisely the awakening of the American people to the generation of racial injustice and prejudices which have plagued the country.

"John Johnson, I salute you and your associates for your remarkable contribution to building a more just and free America. Happy birthday on this wonderful occasion."

Sammy Davis, Jr., one of our oldest and dearest friends, said, "No one knew my name until I appeared in *Ebony*. I remember when *Ebony* started you couldn't get a room at the Hotel Theresa [in Harlem]. And now *they've* taken over the Waldorf-Astoria."

I was literally struck dumb by the outpouring of tributes.

I thanked my wife, mother, friends, and supporters and sat down, abandoning a prepared speech that was distributed to the press.

I left that night for Paris, where on Tuesday a second party was held to celebrate our twentieth anniversary and the opening of our Paris office. The new branch office was on a front street across from the Hotel George-V, the site of the celebration.

More than four hundred diplomats, industrialists, and dignitaries descended on the hotel for the party. The guests included Hazel Scott, conductor René Liebowitz, Marpessa Dawn, and Memphis Slim. As one Frenchman put it with typical Gallic extravagance, the whole affair was one *succés fou* (a fantastic success).

There have been many times when I've had to pinch myself to make sure I wasn't dreaming. This was one of those times. I just couldn't imagine a poor boy from Arkansas and the welfare rolls of Chicago throwing a big party at New York's Waldorf-Astoria and Paris's George-V almost simultaneously. I finally said to myself, "John Johnson, you've made it."

34
"The King of Love is Dead"

It was Eunice's birthday.

I was rushing home to take her to dinner when I heard the message on the car radio.

Martin Luther King, Jr. had been shot on the balcony of a Memphis motel and was being rushed to a local hospital. Nobody, the announcer said, knew what his condition was.

I knew.

I drove on, trying to see the street through my tears, praying, cursing, hoping against hope, but something in my body, something cold and clammy, knew that it was over. After an interval that went on forever, the radio told me what I already knew, that a friend and leader and conscience was dead.

At that moment—April 4, 1968—lights went out in the hearts of men and women all over the world. At almost the same time, the cities of America started burning.

I drove around aimlessly for a while and then went home for a birthday party that became a memorial to a dream and a hope. It was almost as if you'd heard that God was no longer in heaven. And you began for the first time to worry about America and Black and White people.

Of all the people who spoke and cried after the shots of Memphis, perhaps Nina Simone said it best: "What are we going to do now—now that the King of Love is dead?"

There then followed a national outpouring of grief and concern and the unforgettable image of that river of people following the mule-drawn wagon through the streets of Atlanta. I was there, along with most of my editors. We went to grieve and to pay homage to a brave widow and to make sure that no one would ever forget. One of our photographers, Moneta Sleet, Jr., won a Pulitzer Prize for his photograph of Coretta Scott King holding her daughter Bernice at the funeral.

We went through the motions but somehow it didn't seem real. It was almost as if we were living in a dream world and that we would wake up and find out that none of this really happened. But this was no dream. It happened again, to Robert Kennedy in Los Angeles, and we had the feeling that all of the people we hoped would lead us out of the wilderness were being killed.

In the aftermath, Americans of all creeds and colors mobilized to save themselves and the Dream. Slowly but surely the idea dawned that it was "not just Negroes," as President Johnson said, "but it's all of us who must overcome." Universities started recruiting Black students, and corporations started recruiting Blacks for fast-track programs. I was involved in one of the most creative of these programs, the Chicago United organization launched by the CEOs of the biggest Black and White corporations in Chicago.

It worked for a while. For the first time Whites went out of their way to increase the number of Blacks in colleges and corporations. For the first time we got unsolicited advertising from decent, caring Whites who felt ashamed and wanted to reach out and say in some way that they were sorry.

There was a feeling all over America that we were going to work our way out of the American Dilemma. We lived for a short time in a kind of fantasyland, believing that Christmas was going to come and last forever. Instead of Santa Claus, Vietnam came, wrecking the Great Society programs and pulling men and institutions away from the imperatives of the Dream. The grand outcome was a period of benign neglect which continues to this moment.

These were the peak years of the Dream deferred. And in our attempt to create new programs for the new century we need to go back and think deeply about the lessons of the sixties.

This was a time when men holding the highest office of the land said bigotry was wrong and equality was right. For most of this period, we had a powerful moral force in the White House, saying, "Let's be fair. Let's give people a chance. Let's live up to the Constitution."

There was a period before Vietnam when I thought we

were on our way to a Great Society. But Lyndon Baines Johnson and the Great Society got bogged down in Vietnam, and we lost our way. And if we hope and intend to complete the unfinished business of the sixties, we must grapple now with the central imperative—and opportunity—of the twenty-first century, the changing color of America. For the old urban majorities are rapidly becoming minorities, and the old urban minorities are quietly and undramatically becoming the new urban majorities.

For some strange reason, there's been little or no discussion of this demographic revolution in the press. But the statistics and the realities behind the statistics are not going away. And what we need to do now is to start getting ready for the new century by dealing with our No. 1 economic challenge.

This challenge isn't from abroad. It isn't from the invasion of Japanese or Korean or German goods. Our No. 1 economic challenge is internal. It is the task of creating a common American market based on a free flow of goods and ideas across all American barriers, regional, social, racial, and gender.

This is the challenge—and the hope—of the American future. And we can't deal with that challenge without dealing with the increasingly large number of Black and Hispanic consumers who already constitute the new majority in cities like Chicago, and who will be the new majority in key cities and areas in the twenty-first century.

The Black and Brown presence is real, and it is growing. When the cannons fire to signal the beginning of the twenty-first century, Blacks will be:

73% of the population of Atlanta.

72% of the population of Detroit.

69% of the population of Washington, D.C.

62% of the population of New Orleans.

50+% of the populations of Baltimore, Birmingham, Memphis, Newark, and Oakland.*

The consumers in the minority market are important today and will be more important in the next century. For despite unequal opportunity, despite poverty, *despite everything*, the

*Decision Demographics, 1988

Black American consumer market is the ninth largest consumer market in the free world. It is larger than the gross national products of Saudi Arabia, Sweden, India, Australia, Spain, Mexico, the Netherlands, Switzerland, Belgium, Nigeria and Austria.*

We're not talking about a marginal minority market. We're talking about a major world market with disposable income of $261 billion growing to $659 billion in the year 2000.

The meaning of this is clear: the color of the market is changing, and corporations can no longer avoid the two tasks that the forthcoming century has put on our agendas.

The first task is tapping the underutilized potential of Black and Brown consumers. Because of discrimination and arbitrary limitations on free market forces, these consumers have never had a chance to participate on an equal basis with other consumers. If, acting in our own self-interest, we made it possible for them to fulfill their unfulfilled needs for housing, transportation, and personal care items, we could double and even triple our income and production schedules.

The second task is to utilize skills, ideas, and energies of excluded entrepreneurs, like Blacks, Hispanics, and women. We pay a big price, in dwindling market shares and balance-of-payments deficits, for limiting our entrepreneurial and technical pool. Our most urgent duty is to use all our skills, all our energies, Black, White, Brown, male and female, to revitalize the American market.

The new industries and institutions of the New South are concrete examples of what good men and women, Black and White, can achieve by tearing down the foolish barriers that segregate money, ideas and skills.

Our economic future is in our own hands.

We have the power and the potential in America to solve our problems. We can solve the balance-of-payments deficit and meet the challenge of foreign competition.

I'm reminded of the famous Booker T. Washington story about a ship lost at sea. The captain sighted a friendly vessel and sent a signal, "Water, water, we die of thirst." And the

* *The World Bank Atlas,* 1987

answer came back, "Cast down your bucket where you are." A second and third time, the signal was sent out, "Water, water, send us water," and the answer came back, "Cast down your bucket where you are." The captain finally heeded the injunction and cast his bucket, and it came up full of fresh and sparkling water from the mouth of the Amazon River.

We can extend those words to those who seek business growth through mergers and untried ventures and fail to see the opportunities surrounding them:

"Cast down your bucket where you are." Cast it down into the neglected markets surrounding your factories and offices and cities. Cast it down into the underutilized markets of minorities whose unfulfilled needs hold the key to our economic salvation. Cast it down into the deep well of the millions of Black and Brown consumers who constitute the new majority in an increasing number of American cities and who hold the key to the American twenty-first century.

35
The Loop, the Gold Coast and Palm Springs

In three hectic years, from 1968 to 1971, I changed my personal and corporate addresses and bought a house on a mountain peak in Palm Springs. In the process I moved from South Michigan to the Loop, and from the heart of Black Chicago to the heart of Chicago's Gold Coast.

These moves, which changed my relationship to myself and to time and space, were neither planned nor willed. They were the product of a series of isolated events that came together, almost as if they were orchestrated, and picked me up and carried me along.

Which proves, once again, that life is, in part, an accident or, at least, a movement that you don't entirely control. That's why I have no desire to live my life over again. There were too many near-misses, too many happy accidents, and I'm not at all sure I would make it a second time.

My headquarters building in Chicago's Loop is one of those happy accidents. I was happy in my old building at 1820 South Michigan, halfway between downtown Chicago, where I had to sell ads, and the South Side where I had to sell my magazines. But one day in 1959 I got a letter from the mayor's office which said that an expressway was going to cut through Eighteenth Street and that I would have to move. City officials said they were sorry for the inconvenience and that they would give me a fair price for my property and pay my relocation costs.

Prodded gently by fate, I walked backward into a life-long dream. When the letter came I started thinking seriously about my old dream of building a structure from the ground up. I gave Eunice the special project of finding a place on a front street north of 1820 South Michigan. She found a vacant lot at our present location of 820 South Michigan, precisely ten blocks north of our old building.

We tried to buy the land, which was three doors from the Conrad Hilton Hotel and two doors from the Standard Oil Building. To our surprise and disgust, we ran into the same problems we had run into in the old location. As soon as the agents discovered that I was Black, they started backtracking.

Ten years had passed, from 1949 to 1959, and yet nothing really had changed. The real estate industry hadn't changed, and, as it turned out, John Johnson hadn't changed. I went to the same White lawyer who bought 1820 South Michigan in trust, and he bought 820 South Michigan in trust, paying $250,000 in cash.

Then things began to get complicated. Without warning, the city changed its mind and said the expressway was going through Twenty-fourth Street instead of Eighteenth Street. This threatened the old and the new sites, for I'd planned to use money from the sale of one to help finance building on the other.

Faced with this new challenge, I made the profound but understandable mistake of trying to finance the new building the conventional way.

After floundering around for almost ten years, going from one bank to another, I decided to go it alone. To get seed money, I closed the Paris and Los Angeles offices and made other economies. Before the end of the decade, I'd saved approximately $2 million. This would have been enough, under normal circumstances to get interim financing on a $6- or $7-million building. But these were not normal circumstances.

One problem was that my architect, John Moutoussamy of Dubin, Dubin & Moutoussamy, was Black. The bankers didn't say they were opposed to the plan because the architect was Black. They kept saying the building was too much of a luxury structure and "your architect has never built an office building before."

"He's built schools, apartment buildings, many kinds of structures," I replied, "and the only reason he hasn't built an office building is that he's Black. Most of the people building office buildings are White, and none of them have been willing to let him build their building. And if a Black man doesn't let him build *his* office building, he will never get the experience."

This went on for ten years and would have continued for another ten years if I hadn't forced history's hand. Without consulting anybody, I deposited $2 million in the First National Bank and hired a contractor, Corbetta Construction Company. I told Corbetta to break ground and continue building until I could arrange a mortgage at an insurance company. If I couldn't arrange a mortgage before we used up the $2 million, he was to stop building where he was. Under our agreement, at least 40 percent of the workers had to be Black.

Construction began in February 1970 and continued until there was only enough money in the bank for another week of work. At that point, eight or nine months after the ground-breaking, I went to a United Negro College Fund banquet in New York City and sat next to a senior executive of Metropolitan Life Insurance Company. While other people were talking about the dinner, I pulled out the plans, which I always carried with me, and tried to interest him in my building. When it became clear that I was prepared to spread the plans on the dinner table, he said, "We can't talk here. Come to my office tomorrow morning."

This was a Thursday night. I went to see him on Friday morning and he decided, after conferring with other executives, including a Black executive, that Metropolitan could do it.

"That's great," I said, pressing my luck. "The only problem is that I need the commitment today."

"You've got to be kidding," he replied. "We *never* give a mortgage commitment in one day."

I looked him in the eye and said, "You're in charge of this department. Maybe you ought to just try and see if you have enough power in this company to do it in one day."

He smiled and said, "I know you are putting me on, but I'm going to try." He tried, and what his executives said couldn't be done was done.

This was a true cliff-hanger, almost like the movies. I returned to Chicago hours before my money ran out with the

Metropolitan Insurance Company commitment that made it possible for me to go to the First National Bank and get the interim financing.

Life was not presenting its problems in manageable packages in these frantic years.

For all the while, we were going through the trauma of moving from the heart of Black Chicago to the Gold Coast.

One day, in the midst of the maneuvering over the new office building, a friend told Eunice that the Carlyle, a new condominium at 1040 Lake Shore Drive was taking applications. There was one Black family in the building, but we didn't want any misunderstanding. We went directly to the builder, Al Robin, who said we met all the qualifications and would be a welcome addition.

We bought an apartment, and another problem developed. The White woman who lived on our floor—there are only two apartments on each floor—told several people that she didn't want to live on a floor with a Black family. We sent word through the grapevine—although we lived on the same floor, almost all of the negotiations were carried on by intermediaries—that we would be glad to buy her apartment.

Word came back that she didn't want to move out of the building. We asked management if it could find her another apartment in the building. When these arrangements were completed, she asked for moving expenses and reimbursement of $15,000 she had just spent to decorate her apartment.

We bought the apartment and reimbursed her for decorating and moving expenses, and she moved. Here again a disadvantage and an embarrassment turned into an advantage. For we got five bedrooms instead of three and the added security of an elevator that only stops on our floor if we want it to.

Most apartments in the building had been designed by a celebrated Chicago interior designer, but we wanted a different touch. Friends on the West Coast recommended Arthur Elrod, a Palm Springs expert, who'd decorated homes for Frank Sinatra and Bob Hope, among others. We visited some of the apartments and homes he'd done and decided that no one else could give our place the color and pizzazz that we wanted.

He told us up front that he wouldn't take the job unless we agreed to leave all our old furniture behind. Two weeks before the job was completed, he made us promise not to visit the apartment again until he was satisfied with it. The big night came and he called and said, "I want to invite you to dinner in your new apartment."

It was strange and enchanting. Eunice and I and Linda and John Harold got dressed and went to dinner in our own home. When the door opened, I couldn't believe my eyes. It was like something out of *Dynasty*, or Hollywood. Elrod took us on a tour and we sat down to dinner, prepared by a caterer. It was almost like visiting a rich relative, except it was our own place.

People who visit our apartment ooh and aah over the dramatic color schemes and the Picassos and Chagalls, and the paintings by Black artists like Horace Pippin and Edward Bannister. But the thing that impresses me most about the Carlyle is that it has indoor plumbing and steam heat, and it's on a front street.

It's eerie how everything came together in this period.

Even before Elrod completed the apartment, he said he wanted to do the new office building.

I gave in. After studying the situation, he designed with architect John Moutoussamy a great and colorful office space.

The final product was an eleven-story showplace. Rob Cuscaden, the architecture critic of the *Chicago Sun-Times*, said the building "has been boldly structured by its architects, Dubin, Dubin, Black & Moutoussamy of Chicago. And from its broad, forceful horizontals of sleek Travertine marble to its wide expanses of glass, this building says—quietly, simply but unequivocally—success."

The all-electric building was the first Chicago Loop building exclusively designed and constructed by a Black-owned corporation.

We moved on Tuesday, December, 5, 1971, and celebrated Christmas in the tenth-floor assembly area. My mother, who always made a major statement at these Christmas assemblies, was at her best on that day, giving a prayer of joy and blessing that brought tears to our eyes. The next year, on Tuesday, May 16, 1972, we held the official grand opening with a ceremony in front of the building and an open house.

Michigan Avenue was closed off for the ceremony, which featured a moving address by Mayor Richard Daley. The mayor picked up the keynote theme of master of ceremonies Lerone Bennett, Jr., and said it was significant that a company headed by a Black man had constructed a building near the site where a Black man had founded Chicago.

Pulitzer Prize-winner Gwendolyn Brooks read a poem she wrote for the occasion.

I thanked the advertisers, subscribers, and supporters who'd made "the miracle on Michigan Avenue" possible. Perhaps more than on any other occasion, I was thankful for the warmth and support of my mother and wife and children, all of whom sat on the platform and gave added meaning to the greatest day of my life. You could tell this was the seventies, for both Linda and John had big "Afros."

"Thirty years ago," I said, "when we started this company, there were few markers on the road, and the way was piled high with obstacles. Back there, thirty years ago, we were surrounded by dangers, and would have required a building twice this size to house all the creditors and cynics. But we continued to work and dream, for we believed then, as we believe now, that Emerson was right when he said that 'every wall is a door.' "

Today people come from all over the world to study the building, and the most important visitors are not artists and architects but schoolchildren and subscribers who have never been in a building in downtown America built and owned by a Black.

Sometimes tears well up in my eyes when I see the pride on the faces of people walking through the building. A teacher told a touching story about a boy in the sixth or seventh grade who sat in the big chair behind my desk on the eleventh floor. He moved from side to side in the chair and said, "Teacher, I want to grow up and own a building like this."

The teacher told him "It's possible, for the man who owns this building is Black." After that experience, the boy, who had been unmanageable, changed. When he flared up, all she had to do to quiet him down was to say, "If you want to own a building like that and sit in a big chair like that, you've got to quit playing and study hard."

After Arthur Elrod finished our Lake Shore Drive home, he asked us to spend a weekend with him in Palm Springs. We fell in love with the place and started spending Christmas holidays there. On one visit we heard a house in South Ridge, on the top of a mountain, was for sale. The house was a block from Bob Hope's home, and Steve McQueen and William Holden had houses nearby.

Several Hollywood personalities looked at the place and said that the price was outlandish. This angered the heirs and the executor of the estate.

Eunice handled the negotiations with Linda, using the art of gentle persuasion. She told the executor that it was not a price we could afford but that it was worth it, and we'd keep in touch.

When the price went down, Eunice was the only buyer who'd given the owners respect and courtesy, so they sold it to us.

There's no way you can avoid it.

Rich or poor, Black or White, male or female, you've got to pay the price of being human by dealing with pain, separation, sorrow, death.

The fact that it's inevitable doesn't make it any easier.

On the contrary, the signs and warning of mortality only intensify a pain no human can avoid or prepare for.

I saw the signs in the middle seventies. But my mother and I had been through so much together, had triumphed over so many odds and defeated so many dragons, that it was hard to believe that our partnership would ever end.

For fifty-nine years, from 1918 to 1977, we saw each other or talked to each other almost every day. No matter where I was—in Russia, in Africa, in France—I called her at least once a day. On a trip to Haiti, I climbed a telegraph pole to make my daily call. They laughed at me, but my mother understood.

She was the inspiration and the initiator of the Johnson Publishing Company success story. She provided the furniture I pawned to get the $500 to start the company. And I provided an office on the sixth floor of our new building so she could watch her investment grow. She came to the office to call her friends and to pursue her activities as leader of her church and the club women's movement.

She had official duties, including delivering checks to churches involved in our church subscription programs. She liked that, for she had, like all Johnsons, a feeling for the language, and she made a good speech. I always asked her to say a few words at our Christmas celebrations and other company affairs. She said them with eloquence and spirit.

My mother and stepfather, James Williams, who served as superintendent of the Johnson Publishing Company Building, traveled extensively, visiting California or New York at least once a year. After he died in 1961, she was attended by a woman friend, who lived in the house with her.

I'm glad she lived long enough to enjoy the fruits of her faith in me. She always had a car, a chauffeur, and a maid. I visited her several times a week and sent flowers twice a week.

She was a tough woman, physically and spiritually, and she was in good health until about three months before she died. From that point on, she was in and out of Michael Reese Hospital, where I visited her every day.

I never will forget the strange vibrations that made it possible for me to reach her before she lapsed into a coma. I had an early-morning meeting at Zenith that day, and I couldn't, for some strange reason, find the way. I knew where I was going, but the car wouldn't follow the road. I kept going down the wrong street and ending up in the wrong place. I finally said, "To hell with it, I'll go see Mother."

I got there just in time. As soon as I walked into the room, she said, "Son, I just can't fight anymore."

It was almost as if she had been fighting to stay conscious so she could say her last goodbye to me. She later slipped into a coma and died on Sunday, May 1, 1977.

My mother was eulogized at her funeral by historian Lerone Bennett, Jr., who stressed her historical significance.

"She was," he said, "one of the last survivors of a select band of strong Black women who could not be blocked or stopped by anything.

"She was of and in the heroic tradition of Mary McLeod Bethune and Maggie Walker. Like them, like tens of thousands of unsung Black mothers and grandmothers, Gertrude Johnson Williams, vice president of Johnson Publishing Company and mother of publisher John H. Johnson, rose above the scourges of her environment and testified to the indomitable tenacity of the human spirit."

Testified also to the indomitable mother spirit that still lives in me, the corporations and magazines founded on her dream. "It was her custom," Bennett concluded, "to speak at least once a year to the employees, and it was her custom to note that the years were hurrying by and that God had seen fit to bless her by giving her another year. 'I'm still here,' she used to say. 'He must be leaving me here for something.'

"It was with this faith, and in this spirit, that she lived her last days, following the paths she believed He directed. She was following one of those paths one day last May in Chicago's Michael Reese Hospital—strong in the faith, serene and unafraid—when the great heart stopped. She was eighty-five and had warmed both hands well at the fire of life."

Not a day passes that I don't feed off the bread of her spirit. Her office on the sixth floor of the Johnson Publishing Company Building has been left exactly the way it was on the day she died. I've left instructions that the office is to be left that way as long as Johnson Publishing Company lives. I've also given scholarships in her name and grants to the club women's organizations she supported. A chapel at Chicago's Harris YWCA perpetuates her memory.

Throughout all this and on into the early eighties, my son, John Harold, fought his brave and doomed fight against the incurable sickle-cell scourge. On Sunday, December 20, 1981, he died at the University of Chicago's Wyler Children's Hospital. He was twenty-five. We buried John Harold as he wanted to be buried, in a simple private ceremony. Since he liked simple things, he was buried in casual clothes.

After making the arrangements, I locked my office door and sat down and wrote, with tears streaming down my face, a personal message that was read at the funeral.

Many people asked me about John Harold, and some felt sorry for me—I had to set the record straight. I never discussed the matter during his lifetime, but I had to let people know it was no great burden for me. It was, in fact, a joy.

That's what I tried to say in the handwritten message that was read by an *Ebony* editor.

"I am too overcome with grief and emotion," I said, "to read this message myself, but I do want to share with you some of my feelings about my son, John.

"He was as dear to me as life itself.

"Because John was adopted, and because he had sickle-cell anemia, people sometimes asked me if I ever regretted having him as a son.

"The answer to that is no—never. Not once in twenty-five and a half years did I ever feel anything but pride and gratitude in being the father of John H. Johnson, Jr.

"John bore a heavy burden well. He had great dignity. He also had class and style. And because he suffered so much himself, he had great compassion and feeling for his fellow human beings.

"I learned a lot about courage and patience from John. He loved life but knew he was destined not to have much of it. So he lived each day to the fullest....

"John was true to himself, devoted to his family, and loyal to his many friends.

"John's death creates a void in our family that can never be filled. His mother, Eunice W. Johnson, and his sister, Linda Johnson, and I feel privileged to have known and loved John. We shall never, never forget him."

We created a living memorial to John Harold—a waiting room with the latest emergency equipment—at Wyler Children's Hospital. The memorial was endowed by me and my friends, including Princess Grace of Monaco. His office, like his grandmother's, has been set aside in his memory.

Both are as real and present to me today as they were on the last day I saw them. I still have my mother's personal effects. I still have my son's last car.

Eunice and I can't bring ourselves to change John Harold's room. This is our way of saying that he is still alive in us and that he will never die.

You are never the same after a season of such sorrows. Somehow, some way you survive—no matter how deep the tragedy and how much it hurts. But the grief never leaves you and the music the mother and son left in your heart never stops playing.

37
Passing the Torch

After graduating from the University of Southern California with a degree in journalism, my daughter Linda joined the staff, working with her mother in the fashion field and in the production of the Ebony Fashion Show.

Then she realized, I suppose, that I had the biggest job in the company, and she asked the key question, "What about training for your job?" I was delighted. I had never pushed her, but obviously I wanted a family member in place to carry on the business.

With my encouragement and support, she went to Northwestern University and got an MBA degree. At the same time, she enrolled in the special training program I created to prepare her for business leadership. The program, which continues to this day, is simple and rigorous. I explain what I'm doing and why I'm doing it. I let her sit in on all major meetings, editorial, circulation, advertising, cosmetics, book publishing. Everything we're involved in and everything we're thinking about going into. I also send her copies of all major policy correspondence, along with my replies, so she can see how I handle things, including speaking engagements and requests for donations to charitable organizations.

From time to time I ask her opinion on decisions I plan to make, to see what kind of decision she would make. In 95 percent of the cases, she'd make the same decision I'd make. Since I believe in myself, I believe in her and the future of the company. To make that clear, I promoted her to president and chief operating officer. Since her promotion, she has established new beachheads in the new generation. She knows almost as many people as I know. I'm always surprised and delighted to run into people who introduce me as "Linda's father."

Linda's marriage was not a part of the training program, but I played a key role in fostering it. No matter who you are or where you work, children will protest if you interfere with their social life or suggest a potential mate. But I was lucky or perhaps subtle.

My future son-in-law, André Rice, was a Goldman Sachs stockbroker, who'd been trying to reach me for almost a year. Although he couldn't get through my secretarial shield, he kept calling. One day, when my secretary was away from her desk, I answered the phone. Since he was so persistent, I gave him an appointment.

It turned out that he was a tall, handsome, well-dressed young man. He was well educated with an MBA degree from the University of Chicago and a CPA charter. And he was unmarried. He was two or three minutes into an excellent presentation when something clicked in my mind.

"Wait," I said. "I want my investment committee to hear this."

I've never had an investment committee and I never intend to have an investment committee. But I quickly formed one and gave Linda the task of following through with André.

One thing led to another, and they were married on November 2, 1984, in what one writer called "the most elaborate wedding in Chicago history."

That covers a lot of territory and a lot of Palmers and Armours and Fields, but who am I to object? The only thing I know for sure is that it was a big, elegant, expensive wedding that had a warm, personal, family feeling.

There were flowers from countries all over the world, Dom Perignon champagne, and a sit-down dinner for seven hundred at the Westin Hotel. But you can't put a price tag on the feeling I had as I escorted Linda, who was radiant in a gown designed especially for her by Paris couturier Jean-Louis Scherrer, down the aisle.

Special friends came from all over to help Eunice and me celebrate this special occasion. Sammy Davis, Jr. and his wife, Altovise, came from Beverly Hills. Greyhound Chairman John W. Teets and his wife, Nancy came from Phoenix. *Black Enterprise* publisher Earl Graves and his wife, Barbara, flew in from New York. So did UNCF President Chris Edley and his wife, Zaida. The Chicago contingent was headed by Mayor Harold Washington and his fiancee, Mary Ella Smith, and included Jesse and Jackie Jackson, Ann Landers, *Playboy* President Christie Hefner, Irv and Essee Kupcinet, Jay and Cindy Pritzker, Oprah Winfrey, and Chicago Urban League President James Compton.

What I remember most about the wedding is that a brand-new Rolls-Royce got Linda to the church on time and then stopped and had to be towed away. Which didn't matter at all, since the church was directly across the street from the Westin Hotel. One of the biggest moments of the wedding was when traffic on the Magnificent Mile stopped for the grand procession of the bridal dignitaries, who walked from the Fourth Presbyterian Church to the Westin Hotel.

Four years later, a daughter, Alexa Christina, was born to Linda and André. The proud grandfather did almost as much celebrating as the mother and father.

38
Goin' Home

Reaching way back in my memory of dreams, there was also a sentimental trip to my Arkansas City hometown—my first visit in fifty-three years. I don't know what I expected, but I was brought to tears by the Blacks and Whites who hugged and kissed me and welcomed me home. This was the New South, and it took some getting used to, White men and women hugging Black men and women and sassing each other and sharing yesterdays and tomorrows.

What a wonderful thing it was, they said, for a native son to come home in glory after showing the world what Arkansas City folk could do. People who were old enough remembered Miss Gert, as they called my mother. They said it was a shame she didn't live to see the sun of this day.

In the blinding hot Arkansas sun, remembered from decades ago, I relived the lost years with Dorothy Moore, widow of former sheriff Robert S. Moore, and Nathaniel Hayes, an old friend and former captain in the sheriff's department. We talked about old times and old places and called back the flood and the first picture show and the bakery shop, where my stepfather worked. Then we went into the integrated high school for a Black and White welcoming ceremony attended by every major official in Arkansas City and Desha county, led by Mayor R. C. Bixler, Sheriff Ben Williams, and State Representative Bynum Gibson.

I had no illusions about the meaning of the turnout. The people, Black and White, came to see not a man, not a personality, but a dream and a faith. They had perhaps doubted the dream in their hearts. They had said perhaps that it no longer worked. They came on this day to see with their own eyes that it could still happen and that it could happen to a boy from Arkansas City. And if it could happen to a Black boy from Arkansas City, it could happen to anyone.

After the ceremony, I visited the shotgun house where I

was born and the St. John Baptist Church. Before leaving town in a motorcade arranged by Governor Bill Clinton and his aide, Rodney Slater, I walked one last time down the great levee and looked across the Mississippi River with eyes misted by the dreams and hopes and fears of my youth.

EPILOGUE

Two months after the first issue of *Jet* was published, I received my first major national award, selection as one of the Ten Outstanding Young Men of 1951 by the U.S. Junior Chamber of Commerce (Jaycees). In previous years, the organization had honored, among others, Walt Disney (1936), Orson Welles and Nelson Rockefeller (1941), John F. Kennedy and Joe Louis (1946), Richard Nixon (1947), and Gerald Ford (1949).

As the second Black selected, and the first Black businessman, I was the center of attention at the awards ceremony in Dayton, Ohio, on Friday, January 19, 1952, my thirty-fourth birthday.

In the year 1966, I received two major awards that pointed in the same direction. At the NAACP convention in Los Angeles, I became the fifty-first recipient of the coveted Spingarn Medal. The medal is given annually "for the highest and noblest achievement by an American Negro during the preceding year or years."

On Monday, May 23, 1966 I was one of twelve Americans who received the Horatio Alger Award which is given annually by the American Schools and Colleges Association to the "living individuals who by their own efforts have pulled themselves up by their bootstraps in the American tradition."

Another highlight occurred on Friday, September 22, 1972, four months after the dedication of the new headquarters building, when I was named Publisher of the Year by the Magazine Publishers of America. New York Mayor John V. Lindsay, Manhattan Borough President Percy E. Sutton, and major media magnates attended the awards ceremony at Manhattan's Plaza Hotel. In my acceptance speech, I called for new vision to deal with the changing colors of the day.

The upshot of all this was a stronger personal and corporate profile, as *Forbes* magazine pointed out in 1982 when it named me to its list of the 400 richest Americans. The magazine said my net worth was $100 million. Two years later, the magazine said I was worth "at least" $150 million.

I've never counted, but I don't quarrel with the figures listed in the Forbes 400—and I don't apologize. Whatever the correct figure, whether it's the $175 or $200 million some analysts cite today, I earned it, and I'm still earning it.

In the same period, the Better Boys Club of Chicago named me Chicagoan of the Year, the first Black so honored. Governor James Thompson and Mayor Harold Washington were among the civic and corporate leaders who gathered to celebrate what I called a Chicago and an American triumph.

All the themes and stations of my life came together when I was inducted into the Junior Achievement's Business Hall of Fame. As I sat in Chicago's Museum of Science and Industry, listening to the citations, I had a sudden and unbelievable vision of the great names entombed in this Business Hall of Fame, the Armours, the Rosenwalds, the Fields, marching in the same procession with a Black boy who had walked barefooted in Mississippi mud and dreamed an impossible dream.

When I got up to acknowledge the award, I looked beyond the immediate audience and said to Blacks, to Hispanics, to Asians, to Whites, to dreamers everywhere, that long shots *do* come in and that hard work, dedication, and perseverance will overcome almost any prejudice and open almost any door.

That was my faith then and it's my faith now.

I believe that the greater the handicap the greater the triumph.

I believe that the only failure is failing to try.

I believe that Black, Brown, and White Americans are chained together by tradition, history, and a common market, and that what helps one group of Americans helps all Americans.

And if my life has meaning and color and truth, it is because millions of Americans, Black and White, have proved through me that the Dream is still alive and well and working in America.